Zeke's angel didn't believe in love? What kind of nonsense was this?

He whirled to Julia. Her golden hair swirled about her like a halo, and his breath caught before he could speak. He forced words through his tight throat. "You're wrong."

"Am I?" she asked, sounding genuinely surprised. Or confused.

He wanted to take her into his arms and prove it, but he could hardly act on those feelings. Nor could he leave it quite alone.

He reached out and gently swiped a thumb down her cheek. "You are wrong about love. And if it takes me forever, I'm going to prove it to you."

Books by Deb Kastner

Love Inspired

A Holiday Prayer #46
Daddy's Home #55
Black Hills Bride #90
The Forgiving Heart #113
A Daddy At Heart #140
A Perfect Match #164

DEB KASTNER

is the wife of a Reformed Episcopal minister, so it was natural for her to find her niche in the Christian/Inspirational romance market. She enjoys tackling the issues of faith and trust within the context of a romance. Her characters range from upbeat and humorous to (her favorite) dark and brooding heroes. Her plots fall anywhere between, from a playful romp to the deeply emotional.

When she's not writing, she enjoys spending time with her husband and three girls and, whenever she can manage, attending regional dinner theater and touring Broadway musicals.

A Perfect Match

Deb Kastner

Published by Steeple Hill Books™

STEEPLE HILL BOOKS

ISBN 0-373-87171-6

A PERFECT MATCH

This edition published by arrangement with Steeple Hill Books.

Visit us at www.steeplehill.com

Printed in U.S.A.

For by grace you have been saved through faith,
and that not of yourselves, it is the gift of God,
not of works, lest anyone should boast.

—*Ephesians* 2:8-9

A big thank-you to Pam Hopkins for all she's done for my career. You're my own "perfect match" for a literary agent. What can I say? You're the best!

To Melissa, editor extraordinaire.
Thanks for all your hard work and enthusiasm.
You encourage me with your kindness.

To the Love Inspired Ladies.
Your love, integrity and work ethic
inspire me to new heights.

Love always and forever
to Joe, Annie, Kimmie and Katie.

Chapter One

"You marry a man, not an occupation." Lakeisha Wilson made her point, loud and clear.

But it wasn't as if Julia Evans hadn't already considered every angle of her Great Scheme. It was simply a matter of helping her dear friend grasp the concept.

"He is a man," Julia reasoned aloud, though softly. She didn't want Thomas and Evy Martin, sitting across the round table from them, to overhear the private conversation. Goodness knows she didn't want her exceptional ideas exposed to the eyes of the whole waiting world.

It was enough that Lakeisha was going to give her a hard time about it. And if her dear friend of twenty-four years didn't understand, no one would. It was a wretched way to begin.

Smothering a half smile, she coolly shifted her gaze to the subject in question—the Object of her Affection.

Well, not *affection,* precisely, but be that as it may...

Father Bryan Cummings.

Tall, dark and handsome.

More to the point, *ordained* to the ministry and headed for a great career in evangelism, maybe even internationally.

He didn't know it yet, but she'd chosen him for a very special project.

Marriage.

Sunshine glistened off his straight, dark hair, and his smile was perfect and white. Practiced, even.

He'd told her once that image was everything. If he smiled to himself in the mirror to get it just right, no one was the wiser. And Julia would never tell.

Father Bryan was surrounded by a raucous group of young men dressed in everything from khakis and polo shirts to little more than patchy fluorescent swimming trunks and bare feet.

Though he stood on the opposite side of the swimming pool from where Julia sat sipping her iced tea, she could tell he was in the middle of a heated theological discussion with his friends.

In Julia's experience with him, Bryan didn't speak about much else besides the tenants of the faith. His idea of polite conversation was debating the merits and nuances of each of the five points of Calvinism. *With* Scriptural proofs.

That, Julia supposed, was part of the allure. She glanced back to Lakeisha and chuckled at the stunned look on her childhood friend's face. Lakeisha had obviously followed the direction of Julia's gaze, and followed her thoughts, as well.

"I take it you don't approve of my Great Scheme."

Lakeisha snorted. "That's the understatement of the year."

Even as she shook her head disparagingly at Julia, Lakeisha smiled pleasantly at a couple of working associates who'd stopped to say hello. Julia recognized the women as being from the accounting office at HeartBeat, and cheerfully pointed them in the direction of the iced tea and cookies.

As she looked around, she realized nearly every employee of the HeartBeat Crisis Pregnancy Center was here for this Labor Day gathering at the Martins' home. The sun shone brightly, which, with the fickle Colorado weather, was a blessing in itself.

People crowded around the pool, though no one was swimming. Julia had never quite become accustomed to the city version of a pool party. In the eastern Colorado country town where she was from, a pool party meant everyone went swimming. People brought along their inner tubes and blow-up balls. Old and young alike played water volleyball and Marco Polo.

Here, people came to a pool party to schmooze, not swim. They brought their business cards, not their beach towels. It was a different world.

She leaned back in her chair and smiled. She'd dreamed of this world all her life. A challenging ministry in a fast-paced atmosphere. Those around her were her colleagues in ministry.

Ministry.

The word alone made her shiver in delight. She didn't know many names of people here, having only been with HeartBeat for a few months, but a lot of the faces were familiar. Many volunteered their time to the center. Others, like Julia, worked full-time for the crisis center.

There was Mr. Movie in his fancy sunglasses, who worked on the camera side of the video department where they developed audiovisual materials for and about the center; Merry Maid, the administrative assistant who always picked up after everyone else in the office. In the far corner was her boss, Sarah Straight-Arrow, the artistic perfectionist, speaking to Little Miss Muffet, a counselor ever on a persistent insect-killing mission at the center. Julia's toes curled at the very thought of spiders.

Lakeisha probably knew all the names and backgrounds that went with all these faces, instead of the safe but not very effective stereotypes Julia tended to slap on people.

"I'm not finished with you, girlfriend," Lakeisha said, interrupting her thoughts. "Because I'm not getting the point of your little *plan* at all.'' She waved one hand and slammed the other down on the glass tabletop. ''You've gone completely out of your mind, girl, and I'm *not* following.''

''Who's gone crazy around here?'' Thomas Martin asked with a laugh as he turned around to face them.

''Me,'' Evy Martin groaned, rubbing a gentle hand over her burgeoning pregnancy. ''Or at least I will be crazy, if this kid doesn't stop using my ribs as monkey bars.''

Julia laughed. ''Do you feel him move a lot?''

Evy pointed to one spot on her rib. ''This bump right here is his heel. He likes to kick the same spot over and over.''

Julia ran her hand over her own trim abdomen. She couldn't even imagine how it felt to be kicked from the inside, to have the blessing of a little life inside her.

''It's a boy?''

Evy shook her head and laughed. ''Oh, no. We don't know yet. We want it to be a surprise. But we decided early on that *it* or *he or she* wasn't working for us. We settled on the generic form of *he* when we speak about our baby.''

She smiled softly at Evy. Someday, maybe, she'd be ready for a baby of her own. At the moment, she was still working on the *marriage* part of the equation. And that required the *un*gender-neutral form of a *he*.

''Let's walk,'' Thomas suggested, holding out his hand to Evy.

Evy flashed her husband a grateful look, then turned to explain to Julia and Lakeisha. ''Sometimes it helps to walk out my cramps. And the rocking motion of walking puts this little fellow to sleep.'' She patted her stomach once again.

Thomas hovered over her, leaning into her ear to whisper something that made Evy laugh.

Thomas took such good care of Evy, and there was no doubt she and their baby were the center of his world. Deep down, Julia had to admit to being a little jealous of such a close, loving relationship.

''You'll never have that kind of commitment if you keep pushing this Great Scheme of yours,'' Lakeisha commented wryly, as if reading Julia's mind.

Julia bristled. ''It's not like I'm picking a name out of a telephone book, or putting my face on a billboard to advertise my dilemma.''

''Oh, no, of course not. Your system is sooo much better. *Excuse me, sir. May I see your résumé? You've had how much education? Years of experience in ministry?*'' Lakeisha's high, squeaky tone suggested her cynicism.

Julia laughed. ''It isn't as coldhearted as all that. I simply feel that I'm ready to move to the next level, you know? I'm twenty-eight years old, and I don't even feel like a grown-up.''

Lakeisha laughed. ''And that's bad?''

"Depends on your perspective, I guess. Right now, marrying a decent, godly, *professional* man is a critical part of my impending equation. What in the world is wrong with that?"

As soon as the question was out, Julia regretted asking. It was like inviting a politician to share her views on the economy.

"Impending equation?" Right on cue, her friend grinned like the Cheshire cat and raised her eyebrows so high they were lost underneath her wiry black bangs. "Okay, first of all, what is *wrong* with this little scenario of yours is that you can't just choose a man at random—by whatever means—and then expect him to agree to meet you at the altar."

Lakeisha had a point, Julia acknowledged. But that wasn't an insurmountable difficulty. She'd simply get to know Bryan a little better. He'd notice her, and...problem solved.

Okay, a *lot* better. But it could be done. She could show what a great partner in ministry she would be. She'd just do something to get him to notice her, and that would be that. Wouldn't it?

"You think just because *you* made a unilateral decision that Bryan meets your marital requirements, that he is going to ask you to marry him?"

"Not right away, of course, but—"

"What about sparks and fireworks, Julia? Don't you want to fall in love?"

Julia shrugged. Sparks and fireworks were highly

overrated commodities, in her mind. She could live without them, and good riddance.

"Look around you, girlfriend. Right here in this backyard. This place is swarming with young, eligible, handsome Christian men. Bulging biceps and bulging portfolios, my dear."

She gestured toward the jostling group of men surrounding Bryan. "So why settle for Father Bryan? You've been working with the man on a regular basis for months, and I've never heard you say a single word about being attracted to him, or that something was developing between the two of you."

"That's just it, Lakeisha," Julia argued, wishing she could easily explain what she held deep in her heart. It was crystal clear in her mind, but she knew how shallow and stupid it sounded when she talked about it out loud. "The thing is, I'm *not* attracted to Father Bryan. At least not in the way you mean."

"Then why in the world would you...?"

"Marry him? Because he's a man with a future. Bryan knows exactly where he's going and how he's going to get there."

Lakeisha took a deep swig of her iced tea before answering. "Charisma? Under normal circumstances, I would expect you to be telling me how handsome he is. How kind and generous. How he makes your heart flip over when he looks at you."

"What, and major on the trivial?"

"Trivial?" Lakeisha gave her a long, pointed

look, then shook her head as if conceding. Or more accurately, giving up on her hopeless roommate.

"I'm not like you, Lakeisha," Julia said softly, a catch in her voice. "I'm not a romantic. I just want stability, security and ministry."

"Hogwash!" Lakeisha exclaimed. "Not a romantic? What if there's someone special out there you've yet to meet, someone God made just for you? What if you're too busy with your own plans to see God's plan?"

Julia raised an eyebrow. "Oh, right. Mr. Perfect, stamped Made for Julia Marie Evans. Bring him on, Lakeisha."

"Well..." Lakeisha paused just as a large shadow passed over them. Seeing the source of the shadow, she grinned impishly. "How about Zeke Taylor?"

"Paul Bunyan?" Julia spouted a laugh that she quickly covered with her palm. "I always picture that man in the company of a big, snorting blue ox."

"Julia!"

"Well, I do."

Zeke Taylor was a local carpenter who volunteered his time to the shelter. Well over six feet tall, he was blond, bearded and always wore flannel shirts and steel-toed boots. A lumberjack wasn't such a big stretch.

"Zeke!" Lakeisha called, to Julia's immediate distress.

The big man turned and strode back to where they sat, then crouched beside them with a smile. Julia had to admit he had the biggest, bluest eyes she'd ever seen.

His kind, friendly gaze looked directly at her, and she felt as if he were really *seeing* her, not merely giving her a polite perusal. She swallowed dryly and struggled to erase the imprint of his smile in her mind.

"What can I do for you ladies?" His voice was the low, rich bass she expected it to be. Julia had the uncomfortable notion the question was directed at her. He was looking at her, even though Lakeisha had been the one to call him over.

"Julia and I have just been discussing true love," Lakeisha began, despite Julia's stricken look in her direction. "We were wondering your opinion on the topic."

Zeke laughed, and she was struck again by how genuinely friendly he appeared. "That's an awfully big topic."

Julia just barely restrained herself from saying that he was an *awfully big man.* But Lakeisha clearly captured her train of thought, and they shared an amused, meaning-filled glance.

"Let me narrow it down for you," Julia said, deciding it was better to take the bull by the horns, so to speak, than to sit there and let Lakeisha dictate the conversation. "Do you believe there is a Mr. Right?"

Zeke slapped his palm against his broad chest. "For me, I'd have to say *no.*"

Lakeisha roared with laughter, and didn't stop even when Julia pinned her with a glare.

"That's not what I meant and you know it."

Zeke nodded, his amused glance sliding over Lakeisha and landing squarely on Julia. "I didn't believe it was. I was just joshing you."

Her eyes widened. "Oh."

He cleared his throat. "I know I sometimes come off gruff, because of my size...." He ground to a halt, and then continued tentatively. "People often mistake my meaning. My humor is a little cockeyed at times."

"You didn't answer the question," reminded Lakeisha, who was obviously having difficulty composing her features. "Do you believe God has one special someone out there for you?"

"One special woman," Zeke said slowly, catching Julia's gaze with his own. "'This is now bone of my bones, and flesh of my flesh....' She's out there, Lord willing." His voice got lower and richer with every word he spoke.

"Waiting for you?" Julia queried softly.

Zeke shook his head. "No. Not waiting for me." He ran a hand over his beard and smiled. "Working. Serving the Lord wherever she's at."

Julia tried to swallow and couldn't. Why did that sound so romantic?

"You'll excuse me," she said, her words tumbling one over another. "I need to go ask Father Bryan about something."

It was true—she did need to speak to Bryan about the upcoming ad campaign at HeartBeat. So why did her words feel so much like a lie?

She hurried away from Zeke and Lakeisha as fast as she could without looking rude, glancing back only once to see Zeke following her progress with his gaze.

Flustered, she spoke to everyone she passed, trying to make up for what felt like rudeness by being extra kind to everyone she met.

When she reached Father Bryan, she laid an arm on his shoulder to get his attention, and then waited quietly while he finished his conversation with his seminary buddies.

She didn't understand half the words they were saying, and wondered if, as a pastor's wife, she'd have to get a seminary education herself, just to communicate with her husband.

Husband.

She glanced up at Bryan, picturing them together in her mind. Helping others, like the desperate, pregnant mothers who came into HeartBeat. Like the people in his congregation, wherever God led. Who knew what else they could accomplish?

She waited, but there was nothing. Not a single emotion.

But marriage wasn't about emotion. Weddings might be, but she'd seen firsthand how quickly those feelings faded. Wasn't her way better?

''Julia?'' Bryan looked a little put out, and she

wondered if he'd tried more than once to get a hold of her wandering attention.

"I'm sorry. I was wool-gathering."

"Not a problem. I should be the one apologizing for making you wait." He flashed her a toothy grin.

Julia wondered if that was what his true smile looked like.

"I just wanted to chat with you about the new ad campaign," Julia began, though Bryan's attention, or at least his gaze, was wandering elsewhere. "If now is a bad time..."

"Not at all." His gaze returned to her, and he smiled squarely. "I've assembled some Scripture passages we can use on the brochures, but I'm still working up something for the full-page magazine ad."

"That's fine, but we need a mock-up of the ad by Thursday noon at the latest."

His gaze shifted to somewhere over her left shoulder. "I've got class Wednesday, but I'll try to fit it in on Tues— What *is* that?"

"What is what?" Disheartened by her failure to attain Bryan's attention, never mind his interest, Julia spun around to see where he was looking.

It didn't take long to find the source of his surprise. A dirty brown-and-white Jack Russell terrier had somehow gotten through the high fence surrounding the backyard. She knew the Martins didn't own any animals because of their traveling, ministry lifestyle.

At first it was amusing, watching the guests' varied reactions to the filthy animal, but it was another thing entirely to discover the poor thing was limping, favoring its left back foot. Julia wondered uneasily if a car might have hit him.

With a spontaneous spurt of sympathy, she decided she should take care of the dog herself, especially since no one else appeared to be moving.

She turned to let Bryan know she was leaving, but his attention was elsewhere. He burst into laughter.

"Well, I'll be doggoned," he said, shaking his head. "*Literally.* What a crazy mutt."

She whirled around. To her surprise, the Jack Russell somehow launched himself into the middle of the swimming pool.

"What a joke," Bryan said from behind her.

A joke?

Maybe, under normal circumstances. But within seconds, it was clear the dog could not swim, perhaps because of his broken leg.

He flipped over once in the middle of the pool, not making as much of a splash as Julia would have expected. And then, in a single, heart-wrenching moment, the dog's head popped under the waves and disappeared. He sank as if he were a rock.

Panic freezing her to the spot, she croaked Bryan's name.

But it wasn't Bryan who came running to the poor little dog's rescue.

It was big, burly Zeke Taylor.

In a second, he was in the pool, pulling the dog to the surface and into his arms. He hadn't waited even to remove his steel-toed boots. He'd simply reacted.

And saved the irascible puppy, who was wagging his tail in Zeke's arms despite being wet and wounded.

Bryan was still laughing at the sight, which raised Julia's hackles. She guessed it was funny, from one perspective, but she could have no reaction except one—blatant and sheerly feminine admiration for Zeke Taylor.

A true hero at work.

Chapter Two

Glancing at the sky, Zeke stopped pounding nails into a two-by-four wood frame and slipped his hammer into his belt. He swiped in a deep breath of sawdust-filled air, pulled a crumpled red bandanna from the back pocket of his faded blue jeans and mopped the sweat off his forehead and the back of his neck.

It was a brisk morning, typical of Colorado in the early fall, but the cool breeze didn't do much for Zeke. He was pushing himself harder than usual, and every muscle in his body was groaning in protest.

He'd been working extra time at HeartBeat lately, and consequently was behind on this project. He was quietly determined to catch up, maybe get ahead, to make up for the time he spent in volunteer work.

There was so much need in the world, and so little

hours in the day. He was compelled to do as much as he could for the pregnant women who came to HeartBeat for care and assistance. He only hoped it was enough.

It could never be enough.

Zeke blew out a frustrated breath and picked up his hammer, hoping to find solace in pounding nails. The familiar sound and feel of working with wood had often given him an odd sort of comfort in the past.

Lately, though, it seemed he was more inclined to concentrate on something far more pleasant than building with his hands. The silver-toned laugh of a certain blond-haired, green-eyed angel.

Julia Evans.

No matter how hard he tried, she was never far from his mind. He mulled over her every word, reconsidered every look and smile.

It wasn't just that he was attracted to her beauty, though he certainly was. But Julia was different from the other women he knew. She seemed to know just what to do to make a hurting soul smile. She stood up to fight when everyone else was sitting down. She had strength of heart that surprised him, yet a quiet sense of vulnerability that made him long to protect her.

Which was ridiculous. He hardly knew her.

No. that wasn't right. He knew her.

She didn't know *him.*

He pounded five nails out quickly, slamming them neatly into a perfect row. The pressure of finishing the project on time only helped his strength, without marring his accuracy.

Even without this unusual, intense emotional current rushing through him, Zeke could pound nails with his hammer faster than a man with a nail gun.

More accurately, too, he thought, though he'd never tested his theory.

A grin tugged at his lips as, once again, Julia's face drifted into his thoughts. He ought to ask her out and get it over with, he thought. Once she'd turned him down, maybe he could get on with life.

And she would turn him down. Ironically, that was one of the many things he admired most about her—her devotion to the center at whatever cost to her personal life. She must have men clamoring to take her out, yet she worked days and many evenings, not to mention weekends, helping shelter women personally, in addition to being in charge of the center's advertising.

But even if her evenings were free, Zeke doubted Julia would take an interest in him. He was Beast to her Beauty.

Still, stranger things had happened.

At least he got to see her almost every evening at the center. Not that Julia was the reason he volunteered there, he thought, a surge of electricity running through him. He put his time in to serve God and the people of the HeartBeat Center, helping people like his sister, who'd found themselves at a rough crossing.

He prayed that was the truth.

But now he wondered if his motivation for helping out at the clinic had become *because Julia Evans was there.*

Was it true?

She'd only just spoken to him for the first time yesterday at the pool party, and even then it was because of her friend Lakeisha. And yet he had to admit that the desire to see her again tonight ranked right up there with the desire to do good works.

His thoughts tearing him up, he worked frantically, until suddenly he heard *her* voice.

"Zeke? Zeke Taylor?"

Now he was hallucinating. Next he'd be put in a straitjacket. He whistled a birdsong and imagined stars floating over his head.

"Hello! May I come down there?"

Zeke turned around to see none other than the true-to-the-flesh Julia Evans slip-sliding her way down a steep, gravel-covered driveway and onto the job site. Her arms flapped wildly as she struggled to maintain her precarious balance.

She wasn't dressed for visiting a construction job site. For one thing, she was wearing a dress. A pretty, soft, flowery-looking thing that Zeke thought might disintegrate underneath the touch of his rough fingertips. It was a dress that could easily be torn to shreds in a work area full of protruding nails and rough lumber.

And then there were her shoes. High heels from the looks of them, and they were sinking into the gravel with every step she took.

Feeling like a bumbling giant, he lumbered to her side and offered his arm for assistance.

Her eyes widened to enormous proportions as she laid her hand upon his forearm and allowed his other arm to encircle her tiny waist, and Zeke wished for the millionth time that he wasn't so big.

Sure, men admired his strength, but to a delicate young woman like Julia, he knew he must come off looking and moving like a big, dumb ox.

For Julia's part, her lungs had simply refused to work from the moment Zeke jogged to her side to the time she stood safely at the bottom of the hill. He was so athletic, his muscles and ligaments working in perfect harmony. His autumn-blond hair shone like a gold halo over his expressive blue eyes.

She wished she could enjoy the picture, but she had other problems, like being about to plunge head-down on the gravel driveway. Her shoes were the worst possible choice.

Warmth flooded to her cheeks. She was mortified. She hadn't given her attire a single thought when she came here, to this dirty, rocky job site.

What must Zeke think of her? He was all kindness. But honestly, what kind of an idiot wore patent leather pumps to a construction site?

Even Zeke had a hard hat on.

As if seeing the direction of her gaze, Zeke moved to a trunk and picked up an extra hard hat. "I'm afraid I'm going to have to—" he cleared his throat "—to ask you to wear one of these guys for the length of your visit. It's for your own safety, as well as our regulations."

He tacked the last part on so swiftly Julia barely understood the words.

She thought she saw Zeke cringe slightly, as if anticipating her answer. No doubt he thought, based on the little he knew of her, that she'd criticize or whine at having to meet with safety requirements that were nothing less than good, common sense.

Well, she'd do neither, she thought, reaching for the hat with her best smile.

Even though she knew she'd look ridiculous. Even though the hat was two sizes too big.

Zeke jammed his hands into his front jeans pockets and raised his eyebrows. His huge blue eyes were gleaming with mischief, and she was certain she detected the corner of his mouth twitching under his beard.

Her dander rose quickly, and just as quickly departed. What could she say, when he was right? "Feel free to laugh out loud," she said wryly, and with a smile.

A bubble of deep, hearty laughter burst from his lips, though he looked like he was struggling desperately to restrain it.

"Sorry," he apologized when he could speak. He wiped his eyes with his thumb. "It's just that you're by far the cutest carpenter I've ever seen on a job site, this or any other."

"Thank you very much." She curtsied slightly, turning her head to conceal the blush she knew clouded her cheeks. "I'll take that as a compliment."

"It was meant that way." His voice was deep and husky, and Julia looked away.

There was an extended silence while Zeke collected his mirth and Julia collected her thoughts.

"Did you come here about HeartBeat?" he asked quietly, leaning a shoulder against the wood framework he'd earlier been pounding upon.

"No. Not directly, anyway." Julia's chest tightened around her breath as she quickly gathered her thoughts and gained her courage.

Yesterday, at the pool party, Zeke had left as soon as he'd pulled the dog from the pool. She'd never had the chance to thank him, or to help take care of that poor little dog.

"Actually, I'd like to find out what happened to that little Jack Russell terrier you rescued. Is he okay?"

"Tip? Yeah, *she's* fine." He cocked his head and

stood silently for a moment, taking in her mettle. "You really care?"

"I think I've proved my worth with my pumps, don't you?"

He looked puzzled, and she explained with a laugh. "My high heels."

He grinned. "You have a point."

"How do you know her name is Tip?" she asked, self-consciously fiddling with her hard hat.

"Because I named her. Would you like to see her for yourself?"

"The puppy is here?" Julia asked in astonishment. "At the construction site?"

He nodded. "I didn't want to leave her home alone all day. Especially while she's healing from her wounds."

Julia's heart fell. "Oh, my. She's badly hurt, then? Is there anything I can do?"

Zeke smiled gently and shook his head. Offering his hand, he led her toward a gentler incline than the one she'd come down. "Tip will be okay, give or take a few weeks. No permanent damage."

He grinned down at her, and her racing heart stopped still. "Her leg is broken. And I think there's a screw loose in that brain of hers, jumping into the pool the way she did."

"Oh, no," Julia objected, wondering at the squeak in her voice, and hoping Zeke could not hear it. "I'm sure she must have thought she knew how to swim."

Zeke chuckled loudly. "Yeah. *Thought* being the key word."

She met his gleaming eyes, and they laughed.

"Seriously, though," Zeke continued, swinging Julia's hand as they walked, "Tip is going to be just fine. Nothing a little good, old-fashioned R and R can't fix."

One step at a time, he led her back up the gravel to where his full-size blue truck was parked. In the bed of his truck, tucked securely into a torn box and curled up on an old scrap of blanket, was Tip.

Zeke picked her up, and she immediately wagged her tail and began licking his chin enthusiastically.

"You can sure tell who Tip likes," Julia teased. "It didn't take long for the two of you to form an attachment."

Color crept up Zeke's cheek above his beard, and Julia smiled in delight. There was nothing made up about Zeke Taylor. He was all man, the genuine article.

"I made a report to the Humane Society, but if no one claims her, she's mine," Zeke explained tenderly. As he spoke, he stroked the dog's fur, almost mechanically. Julia marveled at how gentle Zeke's big hands appeared against the small dog.

"So she'll recover completely?" Julia reached forward to stroke the dog's wiry coat. Tip had had a recent bath, she noticed. No more dirt spots were clinging to her, and the white part of her coat was fresh and sparkling in the sunshine.

"Completely," Zeke agreed. "And she has a home. I figure she can keep me company, and I can keep her away from large bodies of water."

Julia smothered a laugh. "I'm glad she has a good home, now," she said softly. "I hope I'm not overstepping my boundaries, but if it's okay with you, I'd like to buy a few things for Tip." She paused and caught his gaze. "Sort of a homecoming present for her."

"Things?"

"Bowls for food and water. A collar and leash. A couple of squeaky toys. Dog bones. And a big bag of puppy kibble, of course. Things," she concluded, feeling suddenly foolish for coming out to the site at all.

Zeke had things well in hand, and he clearly didn't need her interference. Of course, he'd made her feel more than welcome, but it was obvious she wasn't needed here.

She hadn't even been sure she could find Tip again, thinking Zeke would most likely drop her off at the Humane Society.

She was thrilled to know Zeke would be keeping her. Tip was a lucky puppy. And buying things for Zeke's new housemate would not only be fun, but a kind of catharsis, a way of doing something now for Tip, when Julia's own inertia had kept her from helping yesterday at the pool.

The longer Julia's list had grown the wider Zeke's gaze grew, and now he was staring at her outright.

"What?" Julia asked, wondering if he was going to call her an idiot. *She* would call herself an idiot. What a dumb thing to suggest. At the least, she probably should have called first and asked if he needed anything for Tip, and if he didn't mind her stopping by the site.

But there she was, the typical Julia, always going off half-cocked, trying to help when she was really just getting in the way, even if everyone was too polite to say so.

Perhaps she'd learn her lesson this time.

"You are a godsend," Zeke said, carefully replacing Tip in her box with one last gentle rub.

Julia felt like someone had brushed a finger down her spine. Adrenaline coursed through her. "What?"

He turned to her, leaning his muscular arm against the side of his truck. His eyes gleamed with a combination of appreciation and genuine male admiration that made Julia's stomach swirl with unusual and unnamable emotions.

Zeke continued, his voice low and resolute. "Unfortunately, I barely made it to the vet's last afternoon, and then Tip needed looking after. I haven't purchased anything for her. I've been feeding her from one of my cereal bowls with the sample food the vet gave me.''

''You don't have anything for her?'' she repeated numbly.

''Anything. Or is that nothing?'' He smiled wide and belted a strong laugh. ''So you see, Julia, you're an answer to prayer today. For Tip. And for me. You're a blessing disguised as an angel.''

This time, it was Julia's turn to blush.

Chapter Three

As the Colorado Indian summer faded crisply into late fall, Julia found her mind often on Zeke. His unconventional good looks were part of it, to be sure, but that didn't explain why she now anticipated his presence at HeartBeat, or why their frequent conversations lingered in her mind long after the lights were turned out and the doors safely locked.

On this overcast Tuesday evening she was hauling charitable baby gifts she'd volunteered to pick up at various community bins, located inside grocery stores and department stores.

During her commute from store to store, her mind often shifted to her budding friendship with Zeke. She was surprised to find they had a lot in common, not so much in hobbies or background as in values, interests and viewpoints.

She realized with a start that she *should* be thinking about Bryan Cummings, about her future. About stability and security.

It was just as well, pushing Zeke from her conscious thoughts. At least thinking about Bryan didn't confuse her, or make her feel all these new, foolish sensations Zeke aroused in her.

Happy and sad.

Threatened and safe.

Give her a stronghold of security any day of the week. Father Bryan Cummings was safety. She would do well to remember that, she reminded herself severely as she got in her car. She had a plan to carry out.

She pulled her car into the Grace Church parking lot. Grace Church had opened its doors to the struggling ministry, given the small, dedicated staff of HeartBeat a place to assemble, and main offices where they could conduct the nonprofit business of benevolence without having to pay a high rent for the space.

The pregnant women who came for help often needed shelter. HeartBeat owned and maintained three houses in the neighborhood, where women in need were encouraged to stay and prepare for their little blessings to arrive.

After their babies were born, they often stayed around until they'd arranged, with HeartBeat's help, new lives of their own.

Julia's heart welled when she thought of the brave women who sought help here. It took courage to admit they needed help, and wisdom to fight their way through to new lives.

Julia opened the trunk and surveyed with pleasure the hodgepodge of gifts—pink, blue, green and yellow baby blankets; fuzzy-footed sleepers; bottles and big cans of formula. The back seat of her car was full to overflowing with diapers, which was a good thing. If there was one thing HeartBeat could never have enough of, it was diapers.

It was a remarkable baby shower, there in her trunk, and that's exactly what it was meant to be.

"Hey, girl, what took you so long?" Lakeisha's sudden speech nearly jolted Julia out of her shoes.

Placing a palm over her chest to still her racing heart, Julia whirled on her friend. "Do you mind not sneaking up on me that way? You nearly scared the wits out of me."

Lakeisha laughed and waved her hand as if brushing away the comment. "You don't have any wits to scare out of you."

"Thanks for the compliment," growled Julia affectionately. "Did you come out here to give me a hard time, or to help me with these packages?"

Lakeisha's black eyes grew wide. "Well, I'm not carrying all this stuff inside, if that's what you mean."

"That's exactly what I mean, and you know it.

Come on, hon, it's not any worse than carrying groceries up to our apartment."

Lakeisha grinned, her eyes gleaming. "True. But at our apartment, we don't have a smorgasbord of handsome men to choose from. Men willing and able to carry these meager boxes in for us poor damsels in distress."

Julia hoisted a box from the trunk. "Lakeisha, you are too much."

"Put the box down," Lakeisha suggested. "I'll run and get that mighty conqueror of baby boxes, just to prove it to you."

"Make it Father Bryan," Julia suggested, giving in to the inevitable. She might as well get something out of this charade.

Lakeisha snorted. "Like Father Bryan would condescend to carrying boxes."

Julia shrugged. She was probably right. "I wish you weren't so dead set against Father Bryan."

"It's not that I don't approve of Bryan, exactly," Lakeisha explained. "I just don't think he's the right man for you."

"He is," Julia muttered, folding her arms tightly across her chest. "He just doesn't know it yet."

"Don't worry," Lakeisha assured after an extended silence. Her voice was unusually bright and cheerful. Clearly feigned. It was an open disagreement between them. "I'll bring back the best man for the job," she assured. "And if he's good looking, so much the better, huh? It'll only take a minute."

Julia sighed and slumped against the back bumper. It would take more than a minute to find the *best man for the job.* Such a man as Lakeisha painted with her words didn't exist. Not in this world, anyway.

It was a busy night in the HeartBeat office as groups of volunteers worked on mailings. The church's new janitor was even mopping his way around the compound. And Zeke was right in the middle of it, making wood frames for signs, his hammer swinging as fast as his thoughts.

But his busy hands couldn't take away the excruciating stillness of his heart. He'd seen everyone but Julia, and he was dismayed to find how very much it mattered to him that she wasn't there.

Fortunately, at that moment, Lakeisha came bursting in the door, her brown cheeks flushed pink from the crisp air, and breathing as if she'd been running.

Her gaze made a quick sweep around the room before settling solidly on Zeke. She lifted one eyebrow, as if asking a question.

He didn't know the answer, so he shrugged.

Apparently, that was the answer she was looking for, because she grinned like a cat and beelined for him as if he were the proverbial mouse. With the gleam in her eye, he thought he just might be. He slung his hammer into his belt and accepted her friendly hug.

"I'm glad you're here," Lakeisha burst out excitedly. "You're just the right man."

Zeke frowned, furrowing his eyebrows low over his eyes. "Thank you." He paused and grinned thoughtfully. "I think."

"It's a compliment," Lakeisha assured him. "Where's your coat?"

"Are we going somewhere?"

"Just outside. Julia needs your help."

His heart jump-started with a vengeance, and his scowl deepened. He was elated, but he didn't want Lakeisha to pick up on that.

"At your service, ma'am," he said, shrugging into his lined jean jacket. With a grim half smile, he gestured Lakeisha out the door ahead of him.

Zeke spotted Julia's car immediately, parked just out the door, pulled in backward with the trunk open. Julia leaned negligently against the rear bumper, her arms crossed in front of her. Her black jeans and pink sweatshirt only served to make her cheeks look flushed and beautiful, even in the muted light of the parking lot.

Her eyes widened noticeably when she saw him. He grinned, wondering if that was good or bad.

"See, I told you," Lakeisha crowed from behind him.

Julia glared at her over his shoulder. Lakeisha just laughed.

''Told her what?'' he asked, wondering if he really wanted to know. Clearly, whatever they'd been discussing involved him, either directly or indirectly.

''It was nothing,'' Julia muttered immediately.

Again, Lakeisha chuckled.

''What can I do for you ladies?'' he asked, changing the subject, hoping to quell the internal power struggle going on between the roommates. It was friendly tension, but tension none the less.

He swiftly decided he really didn't want to know the cause.

''I was going to haul these boxes of baby things into the church so I can wrap them up for distribution,'' Julia explained, gesturing toward her trunk. ''Lakeisha, however, thought we needed a man's help. Scarlett O'Hara and all that.''

Comprehension unfolded around him in waves, and he smothered a grin. ''If we all go in together, I'll bet we can get this stuff in one trip,'' he suggested quietly, careful not to look at Julia, lest she see the gleam of amusement in his eye.

Julia didn't let him off the hook that easily. She took his arm and pulled him around to meet her gaze. She studied him carefully, and Zeke put all his energies into counseling his features and swallowing the huge lump in his throat that formed when he stared into her beautiful eyes.

He was about to break away when suddenly she smiled. Zeke's heart stopped cold.

"Where'd you get this stuff?" he asked, ignoring his scratchy throat.

Taking refuge in activity, he loaded Lakeisha's arms with boxes, then turned to do the same with Julia. He was careful not to overload them—he could easily get the bulk of the boxes himself.

He didn't want to insult Julia in the process, so he made sure he gave her a decent armful.

"These are all from local community bins," Julia said over her shoulder as she moved toward the door.

Zeke was impressed by the quality and quantity of items the community gave.

He followed the women into the church and down a long hallway, into a vacant Sunday school room. From the look of the pictures on the wall, he thought it might be a younger grade. Lots of bright colors, depicting major Bible characters with round, smiling faces and rosy pink cheeks.

"What are you going to do with this stuff now?" he asked, dumping the load in his arms into one corner.

"We're going to wrap all these gifts up in pretty baby-shower paper," Lakeisha said brightly, a cunning gleam in her friendly black eyes. "I don't suppose you transport *and* gift wrap?"

Zeke chuckled loudly, as much at the way Julia

cringed as by the question itself. "I think I may surprise you."

Lakeisha took him up on his boast. "This I've got to see." She immediately began digging around in the Sunday school cubby for scissors and tape.

With an audible sigh, Julia moved to one of the boxes and pulled out the gift wrap. "You did this to yourself," she reminded him, handing him a tube of baby-blue paper covered with big, fluffy white clouds and brown cows jumping over orange crescent moons.

Lakeisha placed the scissors and tape on the table, then retrieved a baby monitor in a rectangular box and set it before him.

"You're not even going to challenge me?" he asked, with a wink at Julia. "How can I prove real men gift wrap if all you give me is a box?"

Julia laughed, the high, bell-toned chime like the ones that filled Zeke's dreams. "Here. Try this one." She shoved a stuffed monkey into his arms. It was brown and tan and held a half-peeled banana in one hand. "No more straight edges and square corners for you to deal with. But don't squeeze the banana."

Zeke, of course, squeezed the banana.

The monkey let out a screech worthy of its real-life jungle counterpart, and Zeke laughed. "That's more like it. Now watch, ladies, and learn at the hands of a master."

Lakeisha and Julia burst into laughter, and he waggled his eyebrows.

Without another word, he measured, cut, folded and taped with the accuracy of years of carpentry and the dedication of his loving mother's early training.

The women watched, wide-eyed and slack-jawed. He struggled not to grin. It served them right. And he had to admit he liked this, being the center of female attention, most particularly Julia's.

"I beg your pardon, Zeke," Lakeisha said as he finished. "I have misjudged your talent and ability with gift wrap."

He held up his big hands. "It's an easy mistake to make."

"I wasn't talking about your hands," Lakeisha admitted.

"The hands of an artist," Julia acknowledged softly, and Zeke stood a good two inches taller.

"You know," Julia continued, "you're just the sort of person I need for my planning committee. The special dinner is coming up, you know. Would you consider it?"

Zeke swallowed hard. He tried to force clumsy words through his dry throat, but nothing would come.

"You really should," Lakeisha encouraged. "I certainly underestimated your..."

"Artistic skills?" he provided hoarsely.

"Gender," Julia said with a laugh. "Don't ask."

"My gender," Zeke repeated dumbly.

"You're a guy," Julia explained, rolling her eyes at her roommate and friend. "You know—all bulk, no brains."

Zeke backed up a step and put a dramatic hand to his chest. "I'm wounded. Mortally wounded."

Julia laughed. "Well, don't take it too hard. Maybe Lakeisha has learned her lesson. Women can tote boxes. Men can wrap presents. There is no happily ever after."

Julia's words shocked Zeke far more than Lakeisha's insinuations ever had. "What's this? No happily ever after?"

"Julia insists that Prince Charming lives only in storybooks," Lakeisha explained lightly, though the look she gave Julia was anything but light. "No white steeds, no shiny armor. Nothing."

"She's wrong," Zeke responded without thinking. His angel didn't believe in love? What kind of nonsense was this?

He whirled to her. Her golden hair swirled about her like a halo, and his breath caught before he could speak. He forced words through his tight throat. "You're wrong."

"Am I?" she asked, sounding genuinely surprised. Or confused.

He wanted to take her into his arms and prove it,

but he could hardly act on those feelings. Nor could he leave it quite alone.

He reached out and gently swiped a thumb down her cheek. "You are wrong about love. And if it takes me forever, I'm going to prove it to you."

Chapter Four

"What do you think, girl?" Zeke asked the dog wryly as he scrubbed a hand over her soft muzzle. "Am I a fool for hoping?"

Tip merely nuzzled into his hand, bumping his palm with her nose to indicate that, in her opinion, he wasn't done scratching yet.

Zeke laughed and continued petting her with one hand, and squeezing the steering wheel with his other as he maneuvered his truck down the highway.

He was feeling introspective today. He had more free time on Saturday. Without work to keep his mind occupied, it was easy to get caught up wrestling with his thoughts. Having Tip with him helped him to not get bogged down thinking.

The more time he spent with Julia, the more he

lost his focus. When she was around, there wasn't room for anything else in his mind and heart.

If he was completely honest, he'd admit he was terrified out of his wits at what he was feeling. She made him feel such a hodgepodge of emotions he wanted to run away when he saw her, yet he was drawn to her with all his heart, every fiber of his being.

Was God in this?

That was the question that beleaguered him now. That, and the fact he just couldn't shake the feeling Julia needed him somehow.

For one thing, she didn't believe in happy endings.

He desperately wanted to know why, what had jaded her. He knew beyond a doubt she was a Christian, and had a personal relationship with Christ. *That* story ended well, didn't it? And if it worked for the Creator, why not for His creations?

He flipped his blinker and moved his truck off the highway. He didn't know what he could do for Julia, or what God would have him do for her. He cared for her, but he was hardly in a position to offer her any type of assistance or comfort.

He was determined. She'd done something for him no one else had ever done.

She'd looked past the carpenter and saw a man beneath. Hey—maybe that was the answer.

She'd asked him to sit on the planning committee

for the quarterly special dinner the staff and volunteers at HeartBeat put on for the women currently in their care.

No one had ever asked him to sit on any kind of committee before.

He was the man people called to get the job done, not design the plan. He'd served a year's worth of dinners for HeartBeat, filling in whenever he was needed and doing whatever needed doing.

He hadn't been sure what to do with Julia's invitation. He'd been surprised, and honored. He turned his truck back onto the highway, in the direction of Julia's apartment. He knew where she lived. He'd made it his business to know, even if it was none of his business, technically speaking.

God help and bless him. His decision was made.

"Come on, Tip. Let's go see Julia."

"There are bound to be some dry times in a Christian's life," Julia muttered to herself, closing her Bible with an audible thump.

Maybe it was just that she was reading through the minor prophets.

Maybe it was just that she was distracted.

Zeke the Carpenter and Tip the Wonder Dog. Lakeisha pushing her to drop her Great Scheme and concentrate on true love, whatever that was.

And in the meantime, God felt far away, as if an

invisible barrier had been erected between heaven and earth, leaving her all alone.

Julia remembered with longing the times when she just couldn't read enough of the Bible. Now it seemed she had to struggle through each paragraph, fight to understand each word.

"Lord, what am I doing wrong?" she whispered in misery.

Julia walked outside onto the small balcony and leaned as far as she could into the redwood railing to see around the corner of the building and get a glimpse of the rising sun. The wood under her hands had eroded from the elements and she had to be careful for splinters, but it was worth the discomfort to feel the heat of the sun on her face.

Besides, it had been her habit since childhood to watch the sun rise. She breathed deeply, letting all her stress go for that one moment. The warmth on her face was like an instant connection with the Son, a reminder that in His arms was true warmth.

It was her favorite time of the morning, where the world was still fresh and clean, not marred by the contents of the day. As always, she wondered what this day would bring. Only God knew.

Lakeisha was a late sleeper, so early morning was Julia's special time with the Lord. It was a good thing she had this time alone, because she sometimes talked aloud when she prayed.

Like this morning.

"I'm not doing enough, am I?" she asked, looking up at the cloudy sky as if waiting for an audible answer, though of course she knew better than that. Oh, that life was so easy.

As she looked back down at her worn burgundy leather Bible, she traced the gold lettering that graced the front. As much as she'd like her answers face-to-face, she settled for knowing she could take Bible 101 when she got to heaven and have all her questions answered to her satisfaction.

The telephone rang, and she raced to the kitchen to grab the phone off the wall. She juggled and then dropped the receiver in her haste to answer before the ring disturbed Lakeisha.

Swiping up the receiver from where it dangled near her feet, she cleared her throat and muttered a greeting.

"Julia."

Once again, the receiver hit the floor, this time sliding right out of her limp hands.

She stared down at the swinging handset, praying desperately this situation would simply go away, for on the other end of the line was the one man's voice she *never* wanted to hear again. Not ever.

So help her God.

"Julia, it's Daddy."

Julia cringed, inwardly and outwardly, as her stomach flipped over and hurled itself around like a carnival ride.

He still had the nerve to call himself *Daddy,* after all this time. Shaking, she pulled the receiver close, pressing it hard against her ear. She could hear the sound of her father's rapid breathing on the other end of the line and knew it matched her own.

He cleared his throat. "I'm in Denver."

Silence crackled on the line, and Julia knew he was waiting for a response.

She had none to give. Her father was in Denver? It was too much to fathom.

"Why?" Her question was low and guttural.

"I've been thinking about you. How have you been?"

Julia opened her mouth, but nothing came out. Her mind swam with thick gray rage until she thought her head might burst. She couldn't talk to him. There were no words to express what she felt.

"Like you care." That was a start.

"You know I do," her father replied, his voice hoarse and cracking with emotion.

Julia shuddered. She didn't want to hear this. Not a word of it. This man had no right to call himself her father. She swallowed hard as she bit back tears.

"Can we meet somewhere for coffee? Please? I just need to see you again. See with my own eyes that you're doing okay."

"No." No way. Knowing bitterness had crept into her tone, she gripped her fingernails into her fist until the sting of her pinched flesh replaced the sting of her heart.

"No? Just no? That's it?"

"That's it."

"I can't accept that, Julia. I came to Denver so we could—"

"*We* aren't going to do anything. Do you understand that?"

"I understand," her father said quietly. "But I can't accept it."

"That's my final answer. You're going to have to accept it. I'm too old to need a father watching over me. Don't try to come into my life now. It's too late for that. Just go on your merry way and stay out of my life."

Quietly, shakily, she replaced the receiver on the phone, finding comfort in its audible click. Taking deep breaths, she consciously shoved the painful memories back into a dark pocket in the recesses of her mind.

She had a life of her own now. She didn't need, or want, her father in her life. Closing her eyes and slumping against the kitchen counter, she ferociously ignored the painful tug of her heart.

"I've got to get on with my life, Lord," she said aloud, but the words just floated away on empty space.

A knock sounded on the front door. Julia glanced at the clock. It was still early for visitors, just past eight-thirty. Still, she was glad for the excuse to push her own dilemma aside for the moment, and she rushed to answer the door.

Zeke Taylor stood on the other side, shifting from foot to foot and jamming his fingers through his thick blond hair. Tip wandered around his legs, sniffing at the concrete landing.

Not quite sure what to do with the man, Julia crouched and welcomed the dog. Tip immediately came to her, barking in delight and rubbing her head against Julia's hands. The dog didn't even seem to notice the splint on her leg. It hardly hampered her movements at all.

"She's looking great," Julia commented, looking up at Zeke.

The big man stuffed his hands in his pockets and grinned. "I wish I could take the credit for it, but it's all Tip's doing. She's a real trooper."

Julia stood and gestured for Zeke to come in. "You're just being modest."

Zeke chuckled. It was a deep, affectionate sound that warmed Julia's heart. "If you say so."

"I do." Julia settled on the sofa, and Zeke sat in the easy chair catty-corner to her.

He leaned his elbows on his knees and caught her gaze. For a moment he said nothing, just stared at her as if he could read her mind.

"What's wrong, Julia?" His question was such a

low murmur Julia wondered if she'd even heard him correctly.

"I beg your pardon?"

"Maybe I should be begging *your* pardon," he said softly, a smile tugging at the corner of his mouth. "But I can't shake the feeling that something is wrong."

She laughed shakily, a little unsettled by Zeke's discernment. Maybe he could read her mind through her eyes. Or maybe she was wearing her heart on her sleeve for all to see.

She straightened her spine and tipped her chin a notch or two. It wasn't Zeke's business why she was feeling this way, and he had no right to pry. She didn't have to tell him anything.

But as she looked into his kind gaze, she quickly realized it wasn't Zeke she was angry with. And Zeke wasn't pressuring her—he was sitting patiently, looking concerned and a little out of place.

She opened her mouth to tell him she was okay, but that's not what came out. "My father just called."

His eyes narrowed, and he stroked his beard with one hand. "I see," he said, though he clearly didn't.

"We're not exactly on speaking terms."

Zeke didn't ask why, but he looked ready to listen. And for some strange reason, she felt like talking. To Zeke Taylor, the carpenter. She didn't have time to figure out the swirl of emotions running through her. She was simply glad he was there.

"I haven't seen him since the day I graduated high school and walked out that door," she explained fiercely. "He tries to call once in a while, but I've always managed to avoid him. Until this morning."

"Did he abuse you?" Zeke's question was almost a growl, and his hands were back in his lap, clenched tightly together. He looked as if he were ready to punch someone, and Julia wondered if he would do her a favor and punch her dad.

Not that punching Dad that would solve anything, other than give her a sense of revenge. But she wasn't looking for revenge. She was simply looking to be left alone.

"No. Yes," she said in answer to his question. She took a deep breath. "Sometimes I wished he'd hit me. At least then he would have noticed me."

"Absentee father, huh?"

"Deadbeat Dad. In the worst sense of the word. I don't remember a time when he treated me like his daughter. He never even remembered to buy me a present for my birthday. He didn't care if I had decent clothes for school or not. I don't even think he cared if I got enough to eat."

She paused. "I don't think he wanted a daughter. I don't think he wanted *me*."

Zeke reached out to her. His hand engulfed hers,

and the feeling was oddly reassuring. He stroked the back of her hand with his thumb. "That's tough for a little girl," he said, his voice husky.

Julia pinched her lips together. "Yes it was. But it's over now."

He squeezed her hand. "Are you sure about that? Why's the man calling, anyway?"

She appreciated the fact that Zeke didn't call Greg Evans her father. "I couldn't tell you. Maybe he suddenly found his conscience or something. Too little too late, in my book."

"Could he be stalking you?" His tone was deadly serious, and a chill went down Julia's spine.

But she wasn't afraid of her father. He'd never hurt her, at least not physically. The emotional scars he left were big enough, but she didn't worry that Greg was going to do something rash. "No. I don't think so. Hopefully he hasn't resorted to following me around."

"If he does, Julia, you tell me, okay?" His gaze pulled at hers, willing her to agree with him. He really cared.

And it felt good. Julia chuckled. "If my dad starts in with any cat-and-mouse stuff, I'll be sure to let you know."

Zeke leaned in to her, until their gazes were mere inches apart, and she could feel the warmth of his breath fanning her cheek, coming in quick, short bursts.

"This is serious, Julia. I want you to promise me."

Julia wasn't sure her mouth would work. Her heart had suddenly taken to calisthenics, and she wasn't sure she'd be able to speak over the noise. "I—I promise."

He leaned back as fast as he'd moved in on her. "Great. Then we have a deal."

"A deal," Julia echoed, placing a hand over her racing heart. Why did Zeke's nearness affect her even more than her father's phone call? Maybe she was just confused, given the way the day was going.

"You never asked me why I'm here," Zeke reminded her with a grin bright enough to let her know he was intentionally changing the subject.

"Why are you here?" He was going to think she was a parrot if she kept this up.

"I've been thinking about that committee you wanted me to join."

"For the service supper."

He nodded briskly. "That's the one."

"And?"

"I'm happy to help."

"You didn't have to come all this way just to tell me that." Julia chuckled. "You could have phoned."

"No—I wanted to thank you personally for asking. It means a lot to me. I...wanted you to know."

"Well, I'm glad I asked," she said, realizing just

how true that was. She was growing to regard Zeke as a dear friend. ''I have a suspicion you're going to be a great ally to have in my corner.''

In more ways than one.

Chapter Five

Before the evening was through, he was going to choke to death in this monkey suit with its fancy ruffles and wickedly snug-fitting bow tie, Zeke thought as he pulled his car into the lot at Grace Church and shut down the engine with a groan.

He wouldn't be caught dead in a tuxedo for anyone, but he couldn't turn this engagement down. The pregnant, often heartbroken women at HeartBeat, many of whom were facing one of the biggest crises of their lives, were expecting a formal dinner, the service supper Zeke had had a part in planning.

For them, he'd wear a suit. Even a tuxedo with a baby-blue cummerbund and a bow tie.

Naturally, he'd tried to talk Julia out of it, thinking they could do something a little less—*constricting*—but she just laughed and told him baby blue matched his eyes, and that he better get used to the idea. As if that were going to happen.

Sighing aloud, he got out of the truck and wrapped the fancy black jacket around his thick shoulders, then reached for the white orchid corsage he'd picked up on a whim.

A really stupid whim.

He was always doing goofy things where Julia was concerned. He couldn't seem to help himself. Thinking of her made him think of flowers and sunshine.

It was his propensity to *act* on his crazy ideas that disturbed him. Think of flowers, buy flowers. Next thing you know, she'd have him buying her the sun.

Chuckling under his breath, he clutched the corsage box in his hand and whisked it behind his back. He was an idiot, but at least he was a happy idiot.

He had no idea how Julia would react. Hopefully she'd take pity on the Happy Idiot, and let him get out of this getup and back into blue jeans.

"What do you think?" Lakeisha asked loudly, if cheerfully, as Zeke walked in. "I look ridiculous, don't I?"

"You look great," Zeke assured her, meeting Julia's amused gaze with his own, and thinking that if anyone looked out of place here, it was him. The women looked surprisingly feminine in their black coats and soft pink bow ties.

Lakeisha wasn't finished. She pulled on his jacket arm to get his attention.

"I look like a penguin. Observe." She demonstrated with the side-to-side rocking motion of the black-and-white bird. "Why do the women have to wear tuxedos?"

"Because," Julia answered as she demonstrated with a waiter's suave bow, "we're offering white glove service tonight. And we're the white gloves." She donned the elegant accessories as she spoke.

Despite Lakeisha's complaint, Zeke thought Julia looked stunning in her outfit. She'd swept her hair up so it surrounded her face like a halo. Her cheeks were attractively flushed, and her eyes were beaming with excitement.

He fingered the corsage in his hand. He'd definitely dived clear off the dock. Maybe he should just leave well enough alone. But when he saw her expectant gaze on him, his hand pulled the corsage out from behind his back on its own accord.

He meant to present the corsage and say something sophisticated and classy, but all that came out of his mouth was, "For you."

Julia's color heightened as Lakeisha let out a hoot. "I...Zeke..." she stammered, but when she looked up and met his gaze, she simply said, "Thank you."

Slowly, carefully, he unwrapped the orchid and placed it on her left wrist. "I, know this dinner is for the pregnant ladies, but I, uh, just wanted tonight's formal to be special for you, too.''

Julia's eyes flooded with tears, though she tried to stop them. Zeke couldn't possibly have known. Looking down at the corsage on her wrist, she almost felt as if she hadn't missed her senior prom because her father had walked out with all their money all those years ago.

Julia's heart slammed into her chest, and she was certain everyone could see the way she labored to breathe. Who had taken all the oxygen from the room and not told her about it?

And she didn't even want to think about the way her face must be flushing as red as a rose.

Her eyes sought Zeke's, but her mortification only increased as he smiled back at her, his gaze taking in the blush on her cheeks and, she suspected, the thoughts of her heart.

Feelings coursed through her—happiness, wistfulness, and most of all, joy. Because of her upbringing, she wasn't a hugging kind of person by nature, but she had her arms around Zeke faster than a person could say *senior prom.*

For a moment, Zeke stood stiff and still in her embrace, and she was concerned she'd overplayed the moment. But before she could step back and apologize, he wrapped her in his arms and squeezed her tight, swinging her gently around in a circle and lifting her completely off her feet. She realized belatedly that he was laughing.

"Thank you," she said again as he set her down. "You've made my night."

He winked and then spun away, bellowing something about getting the tables set and ready. Julia's heart was still beating double time in her chest, but she valiantly attempted to school her thoughts, placing an open palm over her heart and breathing deeply.

Lakeisha, coming up behind her, gave a low whistle. "Have you got an admirer, or what?"

"The corsage is lovely," Julia agreed.

"No, girl, I was talking about the *man.* Mmm, baby."

"Lakeisha!" Julia cracked up. "I can't believe you sometimes."

"Don't you go saying you weren't thinking the same thing, because I won't believe you."

She knew what Lakeisha was trying to do—make light of the situation so Julia wouldn't obsess over it all night. Which is exactly what she was prone to do, she realized.

Some things were better off left as they were, and Zeke's wonderful gift was one of them.

Thank heaven for understanding roommates, Julia thought, charging into gear. Within the hour, she'd put up decorations, laid elegant white tablecloths on the tables, folded cloth napkins around the silverware, and polished the glasses until they sparkled.

As she worked, she made a concerted effort not to look at Zeke. Even an eyeful of him would be too much, sending her heart to fluttering again.

Father Bryan arrived, immediately taking center stage as he began ordering the others around, telling them what to do without consulting anyone about anything.

And he wasn't even in a tuxedo.

Apparently, he hadn't seen fit to dress like the rest of them. He was in his usual pastoral attire, khaki slacks and a blue pinstriped clerical shirt and white collar. He was wearing a black sport coat, but Julia was still annoyed.

Her gaze slid to Zeke, who was seating the pregnant ladies one by one, showering each with attention until they beamed with delight. What a contrast.

She wasn't the least attracted to Bryan, she realized. But that was the point, wasn't it? That her head was making the decision and not her heart?

"The Lord be with you," announced Father Bryan loudly. Everyone immediately stopped talking and all eyes were on him.

"And also with you," came the immediate response from the people.

"Let us pray."

Bryan certainly had a take-charge attitude, Julia thought. He was so firm and sure of himself. And he was always the first to assume the lead. That was something to admire, wasn't it?

Maybe, but it had no effect on Julia, she realized as the prayer ended and they began serving.

"Come on, Julia. These gals are hungry, and I understand why!" Evy Martin laid a hand on her shoulder. Julia stifled a laugh. Evy really did look like a penguin dressed in black and white, with her eight-months-pregnant stomach and waddling gait a dead ringer for the bird.

Julia twisted her lips into a half smile, knowing her gleaming eyes gave her away. She and Evy shared a laugh and a hug before heading for the kitchen.

It wasn't often Julia had the opportunity to spend direct time with the center's pregnant women. Advertising was a background occupation. She'd been looking forward to this dinner for weeks, in order to meet and mingle with the women she served in Christ's name, and to give them a special time of their own.

Zeke lumbered past with a comic grin on his face, and bearing a plate of appetizers like a master waiter. Julia's heart skipped, and she sighed inwardly. She couldn't figure it out. And it was time to put an end to it.

Her future was with a man who served the Lord full-time, someone she could join in ministry, helping others, so their children could see what was truly important in life.

She wanted someone able to support his children—not rich, necessarily, but what could Zeke give his children on a carpenter's salary? Julia wanted—*needed*—to give her children all the many things she never had as a child.

Father Bryan was going to be a famous evangelist. Her future, and her children's, would be sealed. But it was becoming increasingly difficult to convince even herself of the merits of her Great Scheme anymore.

She was pondering her dilemma as she slipped into the kitchen, preparing to take the first course out to the women.

Someone picked up a platter and handed it to her. She looked up, vaguely, hazily seeing the stained white apron and puffy white chef's hat as if she were in a dream.

She tried to drag in a breath and couldn't, and thought she might gag with the struggle. The world began turning and spinning at an alarming rate.

The tray clattered to the floor, chips and dip splattering on the tile around her feet.

She had to breathe, had to speak.

She closed her eyes and labored with the effort to inhale. Finally, gradually, she found her voice, albeit a shaky one.

"Who let *him* in here?"

Zeke saw Julia's face go white, saw her point shakily at the white-bedecked chef behind the counter, and rushed to her side. Something was clearly wrong, but though he continued to take in clues to this strange scene—Julia's hyperventilation and shaky grasp—he was at a loss.

Even more baffling was the chef's odd reaction. He narrowed his eyes and pinched his lips in a cold, hard line, almost as if he were *expecting* the reaction he'd so surprisingly provoked.

A moment later he proved Zeke's theory, unwrapping his apron in a series of irritated yanks and hurling it down on the countertop with a disgusted grunt. Without a word of explanation, he whirled and stalked out of the kitchen, obviously troubled.

The explanation to all this was probably a doozy. And he had the most peculiar notion this was somehow his fault.

He wrapped Julia in his arms to shield her from the sight of the chef leaving. The poor woman looked as if she'd seen a ghost.

But why?

The "chef" wasn't really a chef, of course any more than Zeke was a Tuxedo-clad waiter. He was simply Greg, the new janitor at Grace Church. Everybody helped out on these dinner nights. Seeing an unfamiliar face—or even the new janitor at Grace Church shouldn't have bothered her.

Unless she knew him.

"Julia," Zeke said softly, crouching next to her. "What happened, sweetheart? What's wrong?"

Julia propped her elbows on her knees and buried her face in her hands. "I'm so embarrassed."

At least, that's what Zeke thought she said. Her voice was muffled from her palms.

Lakeisha rubbed Julia's back soothingly. "It's okay, hon. No one even noticed except Zeke and me. Just catch your breath, okay?"

No one noticed, Zeke thought gravely.

No one except that new janitor.

The more he thought about it, the more he thought there was something fishy going on. And though he wanted to protect Julia from hurt and pain at all costs, he had to get to the bottom of this mystery.

"Who was he?" he asked earnestly, his voice clouded with emotion.

Lakeisha glared at him. *Not now,* she mouthed before turning her attention back to Julia.

Zeke wanted to turn and walk away. But something, perhaps Someone, compelled him to stay and see the end of this.

Especially because this was *his fault.*

He'd been the one to invite the janitor to participate in the evening's festivities. *He'd* been the one to insist he play the part of a chef, giving him the opportunity to mingle with the staff at HeartBeat and maybe get to know them better. He thought he'd been doing a favor to a lonely old man.

He didn't know much about the fellow, but he knew Grace Church and the HeartBeat Center did background checks on everyone before hiring them. So Greg, whose last name he didn't know, wasn't a convicted felon, anyway.

It was a small comfort.

And then the realization of his error hit him, slammed him like a two-by-four to the head so hard he could almost hear the sharp crack.

He was seeing stars.

He was seeing the truth.

Greg the janitor was...

"He's your father, isn't he?"

Chapter Six

Julia nodded miserably.

Zeke knelt before her, taking her hands in his. It was an earnest gesture, as he struggled to find words and none came.

"I'm sorry. I didn't know." His voice, low and husky, cracked with the effort of speaking.

Julia's gaze snapped to his, probing into his heart. Surprise and anger gleamed in her green eyes, but not the condemnation he expected and thought he deserved.

"Didn't know what?" Lakeisha demanded, planting her hands on her hips and giving her hair a saucy flick. "What's going on, here? Start talking, brother, 'cause I want answers."

Zeke cringed. "This is all my fault."

Julia swept in an audible breath. ''Don't say that.'' Her voice was harsh and grinding.

Zeke scowled. ''Why not? It's the truth. I was the one who invited him here tonight.''

''Ha!'' Julia looked as appalled as she sounded. ''That's what *he* would want you to think. He manipulated you into this.''

Zeke shook his head, adamantly refusing to believe he'd been duped. ''No, this was *my* fault. I was the one who asked him to come here tonight, and I take full responsibility for that. I should have at least asked him for his full name.''

''He's a coldhearted con artist,'' Julia insisted.

She looked better now, Zeke noticed. Color had returned to her face, an attractive pink shade of angry. And she wasn't shaking anymore.

''Oh, girl, he sure is bad,'' Lakeisha agreed. ''What do you think he was trying to pull, showing up here tonight like this?''

Julia made an unladylike snort. ''To do exactly what he did. Shake me up. Let me know he's here and waiting for me.''

Zeke frowned. Julia had insisted her father was no threat to her, but he'd certainly shaken her up, if that was his intention. Again he wondered at the relationship between janitor Greg Evans and his daughter.

Julia, however, was moving beyond those

thoughts and into action. Her father was not going to get the best of her. Not tonight, and not ever.

With a breath for courage, she stood on shaky legs and moved back to the counter, taking a fresh tray of garden salads into her hands.

Zeke stopped her with an arm on her shoulder. "Why don't you take the night off, Julia. Go home, put your feet up, and relax. Everything will be all right here without you."

Julia jerked away from his touch. "Why don't you mind your own business?"

She knew she sounded harsh, but at the moment, she couldn't deal with her feelings about her father and Zeke, too; especially when he wanted to play the part of the scoundrel. Which he was not, of course, but she didn't feel like arguing over it with him right now.

Zeke looked hurt for a moment, but not offended. Only as if he expected that was the best he was going to get. He took his hand away and backed off, and that was what she wanted, wasn't it? She'd apologize and straighten things out in the morning.

In the meantime, she was desperate to find something to take her mind off her father. She was determined to persevere with the evening, no matter how she felt inside.

Avoiding Zeke's eyes, she began serving salads, stopping to chat with each of the women she served.

It quickly helped her remember her problems weren't monumental in the big scheme of things.

Pouring herself into helping others worked for a while, but ultimately it was Father Bryan who rescued her from Zeke's dogged shadow.

Father Bryan didn't serve, but had settled himself at a table with his Bible, ostensibly so he could mingle with the women. Indeed, many of the women whom he counseled spent a moment or two speaking with him, but when Julia approached, he was all alone.

He offered her a seat with a casual wave of his hand. His other hand rested softly on his Bible, his fingers lightly tapping the worn leather.

Gratefully, she accepted the chance to get off her feet for a moment. She tossed a glance over her shoulder to where Zeke stood, a dessert tray in his muscular arms. His mouth shifted to a frown as their eyes met.

He quickly looked away, sculpting his frown into a kind smile as he engaged a woman in conversation, and Julia breathed a sigh of relief.

She found it surprisingly easy to talk to Bryan, for a change. He immediately turned the conversation to spiritual things, as she knew he would, but this time it didn't vex her. At least not much.

Right now, she needed someone to listen, and Julia immediately plunged in, sharing her hopes and dreams—her ideals—with Bryan. He was a good listener, making eye contact and nodding his head at appropriate intervals. The passionate gleam of his own goals glittered in his brown eyes, mirroring Julia's green ones.

This was, she realized with a backward sort of pleasure, the well-rehearsed conversation of her Great Scheme, the one where Father Bryan would not only notice her, but realize her immense capacity to serve as a pastor's wife.

This was the conversation that would set the ball rolling so that she and her children would absolutely never end up with a man like her deadbeat, lowlife of a father.

"It's nice to talk to a woman who knows her theology," said Bryan, his fine black hair flopping over his eyes as he leaned toward her. "I didn't know you were so interested in the Lord's work."

Deciding not to take offense in his choice of words about the female gender, she nodded, her fervency burning in her eyes. "I can't think of anything I want more."

"Yes," he said slowly, drawing out the word. "I can see that." A half smile hovered on his lips.

Again, Julia refused to acknowledge the slightly flippant tone to his voice, preferring to think it was unintentional on Bryan's part. "Ministering to other people is my passion, Bryan. I know an advertising executive isn't exactly on the front lines, but I'm trying to use what God gave me to help others."

A thoughtful look clouded his eyes. "You know, Julia, you're really quite a remarkable woman."

Julia buzzed with excitement. Father Bryan's intense look created no rise of emotion, but his words about the ministry did.

Busy, boisterous chatter accompanied the comfortable, satisfied guests, and the HeartBeat staff who had now, for the most part, joined the women at the tables.

Zeke, Julia immediately noticed, was not in the room at all. Neither was Lakeisha, for that matter. Probably chasing after her father, if she knew the two of them well.

Julia refused to acknowledge that it bothered her. It didn't. She simply wouldn't think about it. She was here now, accomplishing her goals, just as she'd dreamed, and no one could stop her. It was just as well Zeke Taylor had fled the scene. And good riddance.

Forcing her thoughts away from the strong, annoying man, she turned back to Bryan with the brightest smile she could muster. There was an ear-splitting bark of laughter from one of the tables, but for Julia, the cacophony of voices was nothing more than background mist.

This was her moment, she reminded herself, her adrenaline surging until her ears thundered with it.

The moment.

Wordlessly, Julia reached for Bryan with her

gaze, trying to communicate the depth of her commitment to the Lord's work. Working by his side, they could accomplish so much. Surely he could see it.

But his eyes didn't flicker in response as she'd hoped they would. She focused hopefully on his significant smile.

Bryan cleared his throat, as he often did when preparing to make a speech. He flipped his hair out of his eyes and gripped the pliable leather of his Bible, his knuckles whitening under the pressure. "Julia, I—"

The room broke out in laughter, utterly destroying the delicate, fragile bond she'd forged with Bryan. His hand snapped off the Bible and back into his lap, where he threaded his long, finely boned fingers together tightly.

It was not a nervous action. The crease in his dark brow as he looked toward the center of the room indicated his exasperation more powerfully than words could have done.

Julia turned to see what everyone was laughing at. Zeke had Tip in the middle of the room. She was out of her cast, and dressed in a dog-size tuxedo, complete with a top hat.

While the others watched, Zeke instructed the dog to do various tricks, everything from rolling over to playing dead, much to the delight of the audience.

She even stood up on two legs and danced with Zeke.

The scene was so incongruous, and so heartwarming, that Julia naturally found herself laughing along with the others. She wouldn't acknowledge the annoyance she nursed at being interrupted, knowing it was beneath her to do so.

But after the show, as soon as Zeke put Tip back in his truck, he made a beeline for the table where Julia and Bryan sat.

He grinned, yanked his tie loose, clasped his hands behind his head, and put his feet on the table, crossing his legs and tipping the chair a good three inches off the floor.

Despite herself, Julia relaxed, feeling a definite sense of security when she was with him.

Immediately, alarms sounded in her head. She couldn't forget her Great Scheme. Bryan was sitting right here. Bryan didn't set off alarms.

She couldn't end up as her mother had been. Alone.

Zeke wasn't her father, she reminded herself. But she couldn't shake the fear. For all the good things Zeke was, he was also a blue-collar worker, and would remain so. He would have to struggle to make ends meet all his life.

It sounded selfish, and maybe it was. But she was thinking of the children she wanted to have. Children who would have a better life than Julia had as a child. They would never know what it was like to be deprived of life, though surely with Zeke, they would have love.

And still the fear persisted.

"How are you feeling?" Zeke asked quietly, sliding a glance at Bryan. "Everything okay?"

She pasted on her best smile, but it felt counterfeit, and by the look on Zeke's face, it must have shown. Nevertheless, she assured him she was fine.

Just fine.

Suddenly Thomas ran from the kitchen, a stricken look on his face. He studied the room, and then rushed toward Julia.

She was on her feet, moving toward him with Zeke right behind her, before Thomas reached the table.

"What happened?" she asked hastily.

"It's Evy. Please—come." He was breathing hard and his eyes were wide with panic. "She fell."

Julia didn't ask any more questions. She quietly followed Thomas into the kitchen, not discouraging Zeke when he slipped his large, comforting hand into hers and laced their fingers together.

Evy was on the floor, crouching against a counter and grasping her stomach with both hands.

Slipping her hand out of Zeke's, Julia knelt next to her and put a hand on her shoulder. "Evy, I need you to tell me what's happening. What are you feeling?'' She kept her voice low, even and confident—she hoped.

Evy needed her now. She had to be strong.

Zeke, standing just behind Julia, jammed his hands in his pockets, feeling powerless to help. What could he do for a pregnant woman in distress?

He admired Julia for her strength and courage. He doubted she knew much more than he did about pregnancy, but she was trooping along, taking control of the situation and comforting Evy in the process.

Evy leaned toward Julia's ear, but Zeke still heard what she said. ''I'm bleeding. Bad. I was reaching for something in the cupboard, and I—''

''Okay.'' Julia took her by both arms, silently demanding her attention. ''You're going to be all right, Evy. Do you hear me? Jesus is with you *right now.*''

She nodded, wrenching in pain as she did so.

''Has Thomas called for an ambulance?''

''I—'' Evy began, then stopped as a contraction overtook her. ''I don't know.''

Thomas, bouncing on his heels, jammed his fingers through his thick brown hair. ''I didn't—uh, I'll go right now.''

''Stay with your wife, Thomas,'' Zeke interjected, already moving toward the door. ''I'll make the call.''

It felt good to have something useful to do. He trod heavily toward the hallway where the nearest phone was located. In moments, he'd made the call and was back in the kitchen with Evy. And Julia.

Evy looked worse than when he'd left her, but there was nothing he could do until the paramedics arrived.

Nothing he could do. Except pray.

Julia stood outside the church, barely even noticing the crisp, cool foothill wind brushing the back of her neck. She'd wanted to follow the ambulance to the hospital right away, but there were many details she had to attend to first. They couldn't just leave the women alone at the church without a by-your-leave. Excuses had to be made, at the very least.

So she'd wrapped things up as quickly as possible, explaining as best she could what had happened to Evy, trying not to scare the women. Evy's baby wasn't due for eight weeks yet.

She felt rather than saw Zeke come up behind her. Without a word, he placed his hands over her shoulders and rubbed lightly, kneading the knots of tension from her taut muscles.

His tender touch was exactly the encouragement she needed. With a muddled cry, she whirled into his embrace, wrapping her arms around his deep chest and clinging to him as if anchoring herself to him.

"Poor Evy," she said, her words muffled by his

shirt, which he now wore untucked. His bow tie was long gone, and his shirt wide-open at the neck, tufts of curly blond chest hair peeking from the top. It was the Zeke she knew, and she rejoiced in the woodsy, manly smell of him. His nearness—his strength—gave her comfort, and that was enough for now.

A small group of HeartBeat staff gathered on the sidewalk. They appeared to be looking to Julia. She extricated herself from Zeke's embrace and gathered the group together.

"Evy's baby is coming too early. Apparently, she was reaching for something and fell over. The stress of the impact brought her labor on. The doctors are saying that the baby is coming tonight."

"Shall we gather together and pray for Evy and the baby?"

Julia might have expected Father Bryan to suggest such a thing, but it wasn't Bryan's voice.

It was Zeke's.

With little commotion and less ceremony, Zeke pulled the group together into a small circle and reached for Julia's hand.

It was quiet for a moment after a chorus of *amens,* and then Julia broke the silence. "We need to organize how we're going down to the hospital. There's no telling how long this baby will take to come. Maybe there is something we can do for the Martins. I don't know."

Everyone burst into speech at once. It was quickly decided that they would all go down to the hospital and do what they could for the Martins.

Zeke offered to drive, though he only had three seats, and his proposal was quickly taken by a young couple who worked in counseling at HeartBeat.

Julia wished she could go with him, but knew there was hardly room in the cab of his truck for three adults, never mind four.

She flashed Zeke a grateful smile, and he nodded in response. His big blue eyes were shining with compassion, and Julia swept in a breath.

She was left to ride with Bryan, along with a young woman named Sarah and her six-year-old son Troy. She supposed she should be pleased to have the chance to spend more time with Bryan, but she felt dubious and troubled instead.

The moment Julia was settled into the front seat of Bryan's sedan, Sarah, sitting in the back seat with her son, burst into tears, sounding almost hysterical.

''How can I help you?'' Julia asked softly, turning in her seat.

''Troy was early,'' she explained haltingly. ''I really know what Evy is going through. I didn't know if Troy was going to live. I was terrified beyond belief. He was so small—only four pounds.''

Julia reached back to where Sarah sat hunched over her seat and grasped her hand tightly.

''Sarah, how did you get to Grace Church tonight? Did you drive?'' Bryan's high, melodic voice was firm and reassuring. Julia took comfort in it, and hoped Sarah could do the same.

''I took a bus. I don't have a car of my own right now.'' Sarah wiped her eyes with the tissue Julia offered.

Bryan nodded. ''I think I'd better drop you and Troy off at your house now. Is that okay with you?''

Sarah nodded miserably and gave him her address. ''I want to be there for Evy, I really do. But I know it would be too hard on Troy to be at the hospital for an extended period of time. It's already past his bedtime.''

She stopped and sniffled. ''I'd really like to be there for Evy, though,'' she repeated.

''You can pray,'' Julia said gently. ''God can do more for Evy than any of us can.''

It took a few minutes to reach Sarah's house. Sarah and Troy waved goodbye, and Julia promised to call and keep her updated.

''Well, I guess it's just the two of us, then,'' Bryan said amiably, pulling the car onto the freeway.

Julia started as if a sheer bolt of electricity had run through her. Even her hair tingled, a prelude to her suddenly exaggerated senses. Her stomach turned in waves that approximated nausea.

She glanced in Bryan's direction, not nearly as taken by his dark, eaglelike profile as she thought she might have been. Perhaps *ought* to have been. But she would consider that later.

She was alone with Bryan.

Evy and her baby lay heavy on her heart, but she thought to remind Bryan of what he'd been about to say to her earlier—to pick up the trailing end of their interrupted conversation.

She felt distinctly uncomfortable, and shifted in her seat. It seemed almost criminal for her to be concerned with her own problems at this time. Guilt assuaged her, and she readily accepted the thorny feeling as well deserved.

"What should we do when we get to the hospital?" Julia asked, striving for a way to make conversation, and saying what was foremost on her mind.

"Depends." Bryan neatly pulled the car onto the off-ramp.

Julia could see the hospital lights, and her stomach knotted uncomfortably. "I wonder how everyone is doing?"

"Zeke will probably be able to give us a status report."

Yes, Julia thought. Zeke would have things well in control. Big, strong and compassionate. He was a natural leader whether he recognized it or not. She hadn't recognized his potential until this very evening. She wondered if he even knew the gift he possessed.

Chapter Seven

Julia couldn't shake the shadowy feelings that settled over her as she prayed silently for Evy's premature baby.

Several members of the HeartBeat staff hovered; some speaking together in low voices.

Zeke was pacing back and forth in the labor and delivery lounge, looking every bit as anxious as a new father. He stopped pacing and turned to them as Bryan and Julia approached.

"I'm glad you're here." He combed his fingers through his thick blond hair apprehensively. His face was grim.

"They had to take the baby by C-section," he said without preamble. "Evy is recovering now, but the baby..."

His voice cracked, and he stopped talking.

Without thinking, Julia dropped Bryan's hand and bulldozed Zeke, burying her head in his chest.

"Is he dead?" she whispered, her heart aching with pain for her friends and the dear, sweet baby who'd come into the world a bit too early.

Zeke kept his arm around her, but stepped back and tipped her chin up to face him. His eyes were wide with alarm. "I'm sorry, Julia."

She squeezed her eyes closed against the bad news, but tears leaked out despite her efforts.

At the sight of her tears, Zeke's heart hit the ground. Once again he'd flubbed up his words and hurt someone.

Not just someone. Julia.

He grit his teeth for a moment, trying to find the words to right the wrong he'd done. Words were not his tools of choice, and he floundered helplessly.

"No, Julia. Please don't cry. I did a lousy job of explaining things. It isn't like you think." Zeke's apology was low and coarse, but strong enough to give him the satisfaction of seeing light come back into her beautiful green eyes.

He shrugged sheepishly. "The baby's not dead. Why don't you take a seat, and I'll try to explain what's going on."

Julia nodded mutely and took the seat Zeke offered. He crouched before her, wanting to be on the same level, face-to-face with her as they spoke.

"The baby's not a he, she's a she," Zeke began.

"A little girl?" Tears lined her voice again, and Zeke cringed, wondering if he put them there.

He nodded, focusing all he felt in his heart into his gaze. "She's going to be okay. But she's going to be in the hospital for a while until she gains some weight. I guess her lungs aren't fully developed yet, so she's hooked up to some machines. I'm warning you now—it looks a lot worse than it is."

He took a deep breath. "Do you want to see her?"

"Can we?" Julia exclaimed.

"Take us to her immediately." Bryan apparently didn't realize Zeke's question had been addressed to Julia. But there was no help for it.

"Right this way," he said evenly, allowing Bryan's terse words to slide away unchallenged. With a comforting arm around Julia's shoulders, he led her to the window of the intensive care nursery, and let demanding Father Bryan follow them as he willed.

He moved them along at a crisp pace until they'd reached the intensive care unit for the newborns. Zeke wanted Julia to see Chantelle as soon as possible.

Through the window, they watched a tiny, three-pound infant fighting for the right to live. It was a heart-wrenching scene, and it choked him up even now, the second time he'd peered intently through the glass to see the blessed child.

He shot a look at Julia to see how she was handling things. She hadn't said a word, but he knew from watching her that her emotions ran deep. This emotional situation couldn't help but affect her.

Julia's heart had, indeed, instantly gone out to the baby girl. Unlike the typical infant nursery where the babies lay comfortably swaddled under warm lights, this baby was surrounded by an oxygen tent, and was attached by wires and tubes to several blinking monitors. IV tubes extended from the veins near the temples on her tiny head.

"What's her name?" Julia whispered.

"Chantelle Evelyn Martin," Zeke whispered back, though the glass was soundproof. "Isn't she beautiful?"

"I don't know about *beautiful,*" said Bryan doubtfully, shaking his head.

Zeke threw Bryan the surprised look Julia was feeling. Then he glanced her way, and their eyes met and held, sharing their exasperation without needing to speak a word.

There was no need for words, Julia realized. She connected with Zeke on a deeper level. He always seemed to understand what she was thinking.

And at the moment, she, like Zeke, was questioning Bryan's sanity. What an awful thing for Bryan to say, especially at a moment like this.

"Well, she isn't beautiful," Bryan replied defensively when he saw their combined looks. "Certainly not in the typical sense of the word. She looks like a wizened old man, or an elf, or something.''

Julia met Zeke's gaze again, and he winked.

''It's only my opinion,'' Bryan continued. ''The Bible says children are God's blessing, so I expect her parents think she's pretty special.''

''I expect so,'' Zeke agreed. ''That's where the rubber meets the road.''

Bryan shook his head. ''Where do you get your metaphors, Zeke? At the five-and-dime store?''

Zeke clenched his jaw and looked away.

''There's nothing more special in this whole world than new life,'' Julia murmured, ignoring the men's repartee in favor of the tiny, struggling infant.

''Umph,'' said Bryan. It was unclear whether or not his response was an agreement. ''What I need to know is what room Evy is in.'' He thumped on his Bible for emphasis. ''Can't do anything for the baby.''

And there, thought Julia, was truly where the rubber met the road. Bryan wanted to minister, and he couldn't help little Chantelle. That was why he was so edgy, perhaps.

''Evy was in the recovery room when I last checked. We'll be able to see them as soon as the doctors give her a room. Maybe even now.''

Zeke put a hand on Julia's shoulder, and she marveled once again how gentle the giant of a man could be. His heart was in his touch.

"Would you like to stay here with the baby for a little longer?" he murmured close to her ear.

Julia nodded, her heart stretching back to the baby, knowing she *could* do something for little Chantelle.

She could pray.

"No," Bryan barked, almost like an order. "I want her with me."

Zeke shot a startled and not altogether friendly glance at Bryan.

"I want her to help me out with Evy, that is. I insist."

"*You* insist?" Zeke parroted.

Julia, as surprised and offset by Bryan's behavior as Zeke was, laid a restraining hand on Zeke's forearm. Bryan certainly wasn't turning out to be the man she'd expected. She sighed inwardly. There was so much to consider. Like Evy. Her first inclination, to stay watching and praying over the tiny infant melted away, replaced by a burning need to see Evy.

I'm only trying to help, she coached herself. It couldn't hurt that Bryan had been the one to ask.

Though Bryan hadn't exactly asked for her help. Ordered would be more like it. But Bryan was no doubt wound up given the circumstances, and she mentally offered him the benefit of the doubt once again. This was, after all, the first opportunity for them to minister together in an emergency.

Zeke wouldn't have acted that way.

As she followed Zeke down the hallway, she studied the back of his broad shoulders and set her jaw in thought. It was difficult not to notice the differences between the two men.

Bryan was slim and dark and handsome in a classical way. He demanded attention, and commanded leadership—with his mouth, if necessary. He knew what he wanted and he went for it, at any cost. He was a man of vision, the kind of guy you just knew would make his dreams come true.

Zeke was twice the size of Bryan, and in his own way was quite intimidating, yet she was certain he would never demand his own way. Though he was clearly a man others would be inclined to follow, he led with a quiet, easy confidence she found easy to respect.

More, she wouldn't admit, not even to herself.

Zeke took a deep breath and tried to calm the inferno raging within him. The way Bryan ordered Julia around was beyond comprehension, not to mention common courtesy.

No doubt it was none of his business, but Zeke couldn't help but want to fix the problem. It was his way to work through crises with action.

Hoping Julia didn't notice, he clenched his fist and vented his frustration with a subtle but effective pumping action. That it was Bryan's neck he was mentally wringing wouldn't go further than his mind.

At least that thought made him smile.

Bryan grabbed Julia's elbow and forged ahead of Zeke. "Let me tell you what I want you to do."

Zeke wondered if the deep crease between Bryan's dark brows was worry or annoyance.

Annoyance, he decided, and then prayed for forgiveness for being petty. Someone had to rise above this situation, and Zeke decided firmly it would be up to him to take on that role. But that didn't stop him from eavesdropping on what Bryan was saying to Julia.

"I'm going to counsel Thomas with the Scriptures." Bryan waved his Bible. "You see if you can do the same for Evy. Shall I give you a list of relevant Bible passages?"

Zeke mentally cringed for her as he watched the struggle mirrored on Julia's face. She had obviously caught the inherent slight in Bryan's words every bit as much as he did. But her expression quickly flitted from irritation to compassion and determination.

"I know the Bible well, Bryan. I'll do what I can for Evy."

"Perfect." Bryan nodded in satisfaction.

Zeke spoke quietly with a nurse at the desk, then led Julia and Bryan to the room where Evy was recovering. He couldn't help but note that Bryan continued to hold Julia's arm, nearly pinching it.

Frowning, he turned his gaze away and focused his thoughts on poor Evy and Thomas. And baby Chantelle. They needed every prayer he could utter, and every good thought he could give them.

Zeke forgot everything the moment he laid eyes on Evy, and it was evident Julia felt the same way, as she rushed to the bedside and took the woman's hand.

Evy's face was pale and translucent, making her eyes seem huge, disproportionate to the rest of her face. Her usually shiny, immaculate blond hair plastered her forehead from the sweat of her exertion and lay around her shoulders, wet and strawlike. She clenched her hands convulsively, her shoulders hunched and shaking.

It was a terrible scene, any way he looked at it. But what Zeke noticed most of all was the blank stare Evy maintained. It troubled him that he could do nothing more than stand and watch, helpless to be able to bring aid and comfort to her. He shifted from foot to foot, anxious to find something practical to do.

Bryan was already with Thomas, leading him to a seat at the table in the corner of the room. His gaze shifted back to Evy, but clearly it was more appropriate for Julia to be with the inconsolable woman than for him to try to assist her.

Zeke was no doctor who could help Evy. He was no pastor, to offer words of comfort to Thomas.

He was a big, lumbering carpenter with nothing to give.

He crossed his arms and leaned against the nearest wall, not knowing what else he could do and tired of pacing around.

Julia seated herself softly on the bed next to Evy and reached for her hand.

"Evy, it's Julia."

Evy didn't respond, but continued to stare at the ceiling with hopeless, clouded eyes.

"I can't get her to snap out of it," said Thomas, agony lining his voice. "I've tried to tell her the baby is all right, but it's almost as if she can't hear me at all." Thomas, too, looked pale and exhausted.

Bryan caught the attention of the weary husband by slapping his Bible onto the table, patting it lightly as if the Book itself would lend aid. It was clear that would be the extent of Bryan's assistance.

Zeke grunted softly. "It figures."

Not that the Word of God wasn't appropriate right now, but Thomas needed good, old-fashioned human help from God's people, as well. Like Julia was doing with Evy.

He shifted his gaze back to Julia. When their eyes met, Zeke realized there was something he could do here.

He could support Julia.

Her eyes were wide with panic, and she was swallowing convulsively. This was a tough situation, and she was under a lot of pressure to help her friend.

Zeke moved to the sink, filled a bowl with warm water, and removed a bleached white washcloth from the polished chrome rack in the cabinet above.

Silently, he wet the washcloth and handed it to Julia. Tears of gratitude in her eyes, she took the cloth and gently stroked Evy's forehead, murmuring soothingly all the while, almost as if Evy were a small child.

Evy's shoulders gradually relaxed, and Zeke squeezed Julia's arm in support.

When Evy's eyes weren't quite so wide, Julia leaned forward and took Evy by the shoulders.

"Evy Martin, you listen to me."

Zeke watched in fascination as she forced the woman to meet her gaze, and held it there. "You've got a beautiful daughter down the hall who needs her Mommy. Chantelle can't do this alone. She needs you. You've got to be strong for her."

Zeke wanted to interrupt, to stop Julia from what sounded to him like an overly harsh accusation. He trusted Julia's discretion, but perhaps she was too distraught or overtired to think rationally. Weren't gentleness and compassion the proper tools for this situation?

Evy shifted into a semi-sitting position. Stunned by her reaction, Zeke thought he saw light flicker on in her eyes.

Maybe Julia did know what she was doing.

"Evy, I know you can do this," Julia stated, her voice firm and strong. "Reach into your heart and muster your strength. I know you're feeling weak right now, but you know God uses our weaknesses and turns them into strength."

Evy hiccupped once, then threw her arms around Julia's neck and sobbed wildly. Julia held her until she'd finished crying, gently stroking her hair as she would a small child.

Zeke watched, mesmerized, as Julia took the situation into control, with a gentle reserve of strength and love she probably didn't even realize she possessed.

Finally, Evy had worn out her tears, and lay shivering and hiccupping. Thomas joined his wife on the bed, carefully seating himself so he could wrap her in his arms.

Bryan, still seated across the room, looked grave and thoughtful. He leaned back and crossed his arms, making no move to come to Evy's bedside.

"How are you?" Thomas whispered hoarsely, and Zeke found his own throat clogging with emotion.

Evy smiled weakly, but there was a stubborn, life-giving spark in her eyes. "With God's help, we're going to be okay." She hiccupped and swallowed. "All of us."

"God bless us, every one," Zeke quoted hoarsely.

Julia smiled compassionately. ''With God's help, Evy, you and Chantelle will make it through just fine.''

To Zeke's surprise, she reached up and took his hand, pulling him close to the bedside and giving him a tight squeeze.

''God's help,'' she repeated. ''And your friends' help, as well.''

Chapter Eight

Julia woke the next morning with a tremendous headache throbbing just behind her right eye. She was happy for the Martins and baby Chantelle, who were all stable and recuperating nicely.

But socially speaking, last night had been nothing less than an unmitigated disaster.

She stared dolefully at her reflection in the mirror above the bathroom sink, leaning forward to examine the black shadows around her eyes. Yes, it was official.

She looked as bad as she felt.

Bryan had been furious with her for *interrupting his personal time with Thomas.* Never mind that Evy needed Thomas to support her, and that things moved forward rapidly from there.

Did it matter at all to him that Evy was doing

much better, and that Chantelle was holding her own?

As if his insult wasn't enough, he'd kept up a sulky silence the whole drive home. She was beginning to feel Bryan, the man she'd carefully selected to marry based on a specific and rigid set of criteria, was actually nothing more than a spoiled child.

Maybe she'd just picked the wrong pastor. Surely there were others not quite so full of themselves. It figured she'd picked Bryan. He just hadn't been that great at the hospital.

The clear winner in the respect department was Zeke, who'd been calm and strong all night long. And when she'd needed him, he'd been there for her, no questions asked. She had a connection with him, something internal and impossible to explain. But she didn't want to marry him.

Someone thumped several times on the door, and the pain in Julia's head hammered sharply with every knock, swelling like a tidal wave and making her insides dip and sway.

Julia groaned and shuffled back toward the bedroom. Whoever it was would just have to wait. But of course, whoever it was promptly began another round of persistent banging.

"I'm coming, I'm coming," she howled, glaring in the direction of the front door. She tossed on a pair of purple sweatpants and an ripped old blue T-shirt, then moved toward the bathroom, thinking to at least run a brush through her tousled locks before answering the door.

She stomped to the door and swung it open. It took less than one second for her to realize her day had definitely gone from bad to worse.

Father Bryan stood glaring, arms crossed and feet braced, in the threshold. There was an agonizing moment as his gaze took in her hair and mussed clothes, his face expressionless.

When their eyes met, she realized with horror she was still wearing the remnants of yesterday's mascara. She cringed. She didn't suppose is could get much worse than this.

Bryan didn't smile. His lips slowly turned down at the corners, as if he'd sampled some food that disagreed with him. His overall demeanor suggested someone had gone and ruined his perfectly good day.

Probably her.

She winced, and her face flamed. She brushed her hair down with the flat of her hand, only to feel it *poing* back up to its original points with resolute tenacity.

Just as quickly as it had appeared, her embarrassment faded, her hackles raised with righteous indignation.

What had ever possessed her to consider Father Bryan Cummings as marriage material? He was a conceited snob who only thought of ministry as it benefited his own career, or his ego.

She wanted to shake herself for being so daft as to even consider planning so dire a fate as marrying a man like Bryan. She almost shivered. What had she been thinking?

It was then that she saw Zeke. He stood just behind Bryan, his arms loaded with boxes.

Zeke's blue eyes gleamed with amusement, the corner of his mouth twitching as he struggled to keep his even features composed.

If that man laughs at me, I swear I'm going to scream, Julia thought, once more wallowing in embarrassment, but appreciating the smile his humor brought to her lips. She looked from one man to the other and experienced the fleeting childish desire to stick out her tongue at the both of them.

With that thought in mind, she smiled.

Zeke smiled back at her as if sharing the joke. Bryan continued to scowl.

Under the circumstances, she could only think of one viable alternative.

She closed the door. Hard.

Zeke snickered.

"What are you laughing at?" Bryan barked, turning to face Zeke with a scowl. "I hardly think this is a funny situation."

Zeke divested himself of the boxes he held, squatted down against the opposite wall, pulled his baseball cap low on his forehead and settled in to wait. He'd wait all day for sweet Julia.

In freezing drizzle. Fortunately, the day was partly cloudy and not too unbearably cold.

Zeke ran a hand down the beard on his cheek and tried not to smile. "To have the door slammed in my face by a beautiful woman? I think it's hilarious."

Bryan grunted and shifted from one foot to the other. He didn't say it, but Zeke could see the *you would* in his stance and gaze.

"We didn't call first," Zeke reminded him, though he knew his logic fell on deaf ears.

"What does she expect us to do out here? Just stand here and freeze until she deems to open the door again for us?"

Again, Zeke couldn't help but laugh. "Pretty much."

Bryan grumbled under his breath and leaned his shoulder against the door.

Five minutes later, Julia opened the door, welcoming them in with a singsong voice.

Bryan, who'd leaned his full weight against the door, catapulted into the room, stopping just short of a somersault on the living room floor.

Zeke yawned and stretched, giving the impression of a man ready to nod off to sleep. But when Julia approached, he smiled and extended his hand. "Help me up?"

"As if I could," she said, laughing, but she reached for his hand. He pulled himself up, giving her hand a quick squeeze before releasing it.

Their eyes met and held. Zeke's mouth went dry and he couldn't swallow. He cleared his throat. "I'll just get these boxes. Will you hold the door?"

He was aware of her watching as he carefully and single-handedly balanced three large boxes in his arms, praying they wouldn't tip over and make a fool of him. The boxes were loaded to the brim, and he sure didn't want to crash and burn in front of Julia.

Bryan didn't offer to help, of course, except for directing Zeke to put the boxes in the kitchen. Zeke didn't take offense—it wasn't worth the mental energy to bother.

Julia cornered him as he stacked the boxes neatly on the kitchen counter. "Okay, guys, what's this all about? Or am I supposed to guess?"

"Where's Lakeisha?" Bryan asked, ignoring Julia's question. He peered down the hallway curiously. "Is she still sleeping?"

"Lakeisha?" Julia repeated. "She is still sound asleep. We won't see her until noon at the least."

Zeke chuckled. "A night owl, huh?"

"Classic case. I think she was up until after 2:00 a.m. reading."

"Well, that complicates things," Bryan said, sounding annoyed. Which he probably was, Zeke thought. Every little thing bothered the man, if it was out of his control.

"Bryan, the ladies had no way of knowing we were coming," Zeke reminded him in a stage whisper.

He flashed Julia an apologetic smile. "Bryan and I were trying to think up some practical ways we could help the Martins. We thought you and Lakeisha could help us brainstorm." He waggled his eyebrows. "Give us a female viewpoint, you know?"

Julia chuckled. She was still unsettled about the men's unannounced appearance at her door, not to mention being disconcerted by the casual, all-male way Zeke leaned on the kitchen counter, looking adorable with his ruffled hair and sleek beard. He looked as if he belonged there, in her kitchen, every bit as comfortable as her salt and pepper shakers and the cookie jar.

Only infinitely more dangerous.

"I'm free today to help you, but I can't speak for Lakeisha, since I don't know if she's made plans for the day."

She peered through the hand hole of the nearest box. "What's in here?"

Zeke lifted the lid on the first box, which was heavily laden with food—a bag of flour, one of sugar and a box of biscuit mix. The second box contained milk, eggs, bread, meat and other perishables. The third box wasn't covered, and contained laundry soap, disinfectant and a whole host of cleaning supplies.

"We wanted you ladies to see what we'd acquired, so you could give us advice on what you still needed."

Bryan took a seat at the head of the table and threaded his fingers together. "Seeing as I'm the minister here, I'll be in charge of this operation," he proclaimed out of nowhere.

"What operation?" asked Julia, confused.

"Operation Baby Chantelle, of course," said Zeke with a chuckle.

Julia grinned at him as the idea sank in.

"Could we please be serious here?" Bryan exclaimed, his melodic tenor sounding stilted, as if he were clenching his teeth.

"Sorry," said Zeke, looking adorably repentant as he slid a wink at Julia.

"We're on our way to the Martins'. We thought we could cook and clean or...something," Bryan finished slowly.

"Do either of you men know how to cook?" Julia queried.

"Well, no, of course not," said Bryan. "That's why you and Lakeisha have to come with us."

"Speak for yourself," howled Zeke, sounding

genuinely offended. He pulled himself up to his full well over six-foot height and pulled on the collar of his blue-plaid flannel like a man preparing to give a speech. "I'll have you know that I'm an outstanding gourmet cook. Though we probably won't be cooking any gourmet meals today."

"It's a good thing you can cook, Mr. Gourmet," said Julia with a laugh, "because I can't boil water."

"You...can't?" She wished Bryan didn't sound quite so flabbergasted. It wasn't the Dark Ages, for crying out loud. Hadn't he ever heard of *take-out?*

"I'm a firm believer in fast food and the supermarket deli section, if you must know," she explained reluctantly.

Bryan shook his head, as if he couldn't believe her words. "Well, cook or no cook, we're planning to meet at the Martins' house this afternoon. We want you and Lakeisha to join us." He sounded as if the issue with Lakeisha were settled, if not to his satisfaction, then at least as best as possible.

"Again, I can't speak for Lakeisha, but I'll be there." Julia paused and swept her hair back with her hand. "Any updates on Chantelle?"

Zeke nodded. "I called the hospital this morning. She appears to be holding her own. But we need to keep praying."

"I'm glad you thought to include me in your mercy mission," she said softly, catching Zeke's eye. She knew this operation wasn't the brainchild of Father Bryan, no matter how he scowled at being left out.

She smiled, trying to include a sulky Bryan in the gesture, but her gaze continued to be locked with Zeke's. Completely unnerved, she strove to continue her dialogue. "It helps to have something constructive to do."

"Yes, it does," Zeke agreed with a smile that was for her alone. It made her toes curl.

"I guess I can pack up these boxes, then, since you can't help me with recipes." He winked at Julia before replacing the covers on the boxes and bundling them into his arms. "See you this afternoon."

Julia's breath caught. "Of course."

It was like a huge, blaring signpost that Bryan didn't offer to help Zeke carry anything. He merely tucked his ever present Bible underneath his arm and waved a hand at Julia. Zeke might have been a burro, for all the attention Bryan paid him.

Julia bristled. She tried to play the good hostess and smile, but knew that with Bryan it was more like a grimace. She had a lot of thinking to do, where Father Bryan was concerned. But right now, she just wanted everyone out of the apartment so she could have some room to reflect on recent circumstances.

"Until this afternoon, then," she said cordially, then shut the door and leaned against it with a sigh.

She hoped Lakeisha would decide to come with her. She didn't know if she could spend an entire afternoon in the company of Zeke and Bryan without going completely crazy.

As if thinking about her had wakened her, Lakeisha appeared in the kitchen, yawning and rubbing her eyes. She took a good look at Julia and chuckled.

"And I thought I had a late night." Lakeisha flopped onto the sofa and stretched. "Who was that at the door?"

"Would you believe it was Father Bryan and Zeke Taylor? They wanted to enlist our help cleaning and cooking for the Martins this afternoon."

"Ha," Lakeisha snorted. "They obviously don't know of your considerable talent in the culinary field."

Julia sniffed and stuck her nose in the air. "I informed them of my...deficiencies. And they want me anyway."

Lakeisha raised her eyebrows. "I'm sure they do."

Julia blushed. "That's not what I meant and you know it." She flopped down in the armchair across from the couch, tucking one knee up under her. "You may be interested to hear I have officially given up on the Great Scheme."

That got Lakeisha's attention. "Yeah? I'm ecstatic. You've finally come to your senses."

Julia shook her head. ''It's simply that I've decided Bryan and I are...incompatible.''

Lakeisha roared with laughter. ''Now that's an understatement if I ever heard one.''

''So do you want to come with me today, or what?'' Julia asked, quickly changing the subject.

''Poor Evy,'' Lakeisha said. ''I'd be glad to have something constructive to do for her.''

''Me, too. I always feel like my hands are tied in these kinds of situations. My heart goes out to them so much, but I can't do anything to ease their pain.''

''You said Zeke will be there today?'' Lakeisha asked just a touch too brightly. Julia didn't blame her. It was hard to think about Evy's situation.

''Yes. Why?''

Lakeisha gave her a pointed look. ''Why do you think?''

''Can we not go there?'' Julia asked, irritated.

''Oh, stop being grumpy,'' Lakeisha replied lightly. ''Do you like him, or don't you?''

It certainly didn't take any effort to conjure up his handsome face. ''He's okay,'' she agreed reluctantly. Julia studied her cuticles in order to avoid meeting Lakeisha's eyes.

''Better or worse than chopped liver?''

''Oh Lakeisha,'' Julia exclaimed, laughing. ''I like Zeke okay. It's just that...''

What? Just what?

''Just?'' Lakeisha prompted.

"He's just too much like Daddy—um, like my father." A spark of anger went through her at the thought of her encounter with her father last night, but she pushed it aside.

"Big, brawny, delicious Zeke? Mmm-mmm, girlfriend, not even close. How do you mean, like your *father?*"

"Oh, I don't know," Julia admitted with a sigh. "His job. Mostly. I guess."

"Zeke's a carpenter, for crying out loud," Lakeisha squeaked, sounding exasperated. "How is that anything remotely like a deadbeat dad?"

"He's a blue-collar worker," Julia replied promptly, knowing very well how judgmental and thickheaded her answer sounded. "I can't help the way I feel, Lakeisha. I know it's dumb, but I've always had it in my head to marry a minister. Who better to raise my kids. I don't want my children's lives to turn out like mine did with my blue-collar worker dad. I couldn't live with myself if that happened."

"I can't fault you there, girlfriend," Lakeisha said earnestly. "And I sure won't be the one to throw the first stone."

Julia sighed inwardly. Clearly Bryan wasn't the hoped-for answer to her problems, but now she didn't know if there was an answer. At least with Bryan there'd been a pitiful sense of hope. There were other pastors, she supposed, but right now that sounded like a pretty grim prospect.

All she felt now with regard to plans for her future was a vast, gaping emptiness.

Was that what she had to look forward to? Emptiness?

Without Bryan, she'd probably fall head over heels in love, and get married for all the *right* reasons.

And then die miserably when the love of her life found greener pastures and moved on.

Like her mother died at the uncaring hand of her father.

A feeling—not butterflies, but more like a family of kangaroos—bounced around in her stomach in every which direction.

She couldn't let herself fall in love.

Chapter Nine

It was difficult to understand God's ways sometimes, Zeke thought as he sat straight-backed on the edge of the Martins' couch. He knew it sounded like a cop-out to some, but he believed everything God did was for good. Even the early and traumatic arrival of baby Chantelle was nestled in the hands of a loving God.

It was just that God didn't always explain His motives. Like when a parent said *"Because I said so,"* to an unruly child who didn't know what was really best for himself.

But it was hard to swallow even with faith, and he wondered how Evy and Thomas were coping. He also wondered where Julia and Lakeisha had gone. He shifted uncomfortably and rested his arms on his knees.

He jumped and bounded to the front door when he heard Lakeisha impatiently pounding on it with her fist. ''Get out the scrubbers and cleaners—your work crew is here!''

Zeke immediately opened the front door and gestured her in, his heart not settled until his darting gaze landed on Julia and affirmed she was present. ''I'm glad you're here,'' he said sincerely. ''I was beginning to think no one was going to show up.''

''What, and miss the party?'' Julia joked, tugging on the hem of her purple sweatshirt.

''Speaking of which,'' Lakeisha added, ''Where *is* the party?''

Zeke shrugged. ''A group of ladies from HeartBeat came in and whisked through the house with the cleaning stuff. Not that there was much to do. Evy keeps her house spotless.''

Julia's face fell. ''Oh, then there's nothing left to do to help Evy?''

Zeke ran a hand along her shoulder. ''Sure there is. Actually, we get the good stuff—the real practical part of the job that will make a difference for Evy when she gets home.''

''Where's Father Bryan?'' Lakeisha asked.

Zeke noticed the pointed look she gave Julia, but brushed it off as nothing. He wasn't into the mind-reading business. He grinned wryly. ''Bryan decided his talents lent themselves to reading the Scriptures with Evy and Thomas at the hospital.

Lakeisha barked out a laugh. ''Now, why am I not surprised? Scrubbing toilets is just not within Father Bryan's capacity.''

Zeke agreed. The Martins needed grunt labor to help them out today. And that, Zeke would bet, were he a betting man, was something Father Bryan Cummings would never condescend to do.

For the first time, it bothered Zeke a little that he *was* the kind of man people called when they needed handiwork done.

And for a brief moment, he admitted, if only to himself, that he was jealous.

Father Bryan was the kind of man Julia would want to spend her life with—a slick, well-dressed young man with a great education and a good future ahead of him.

Zeke couldn't hold a candle to him. Not in looks, for sure. He was nothing but a bumbling giant in dirty work clothes. The only future he could give a woman was love. No fantastic career. No big nest egg for retirement, though he had some money tucked away.

Sweet Julia deserved so much more than he could ever hope to offer.

He frowned and stroked his beard. When had this dream formed, the one where he and Julia could be together? He'd been happy with his life as it was, and hadn't really considered how it might look to a woman. To Julia.

His head was swimming with emotion by the time he reached Julia, and he didn't know what to do. He wasn't used to experiencing emotion with any particular depth, and certainly nothing in his scope of his experience had ever compared to this. He was a man of action.

But when he was with Julia, he didn't know his head from his toe, a jigsaw from a chain saw, or even which end of the nail to pound. He felt stone stupid and soaringly brilliant all at the same time.

Zeke mentally shook himself back to the present moment and the work ahead of him. "Do you want to flip for chores? Heads I do laundry, tails I cook. What do you think?"

His gaze was aimed at Julia, but Lakeisha quickly broke in. "I think you'd better come up tails, Zeke, or Evy's going to get a week of boxed dinners."

He chuckled. "Okay, then, ladies, let me help you find the washer and dryer."

"Well, that should do it," said Julia, wiping a drop of perspiration off her temple with the corner of her oversize sweatshirt.

The Martins' laundry room was nothing more than a small, drywalled corner without even a single window to shed light. The sixty-watt bulb dangling from the open socket overhead did little to illuminate the humid darkness.

"One load to go, and we're out of here. I never

knew folding cloth diapers could be so tedious. Can you imagine having to do this every other day? I can't imagine why Evy chose cloth diapers. I'd have a diaper service, at least.'' She chuckled.

''I hope Zeke is faring better than we are,'' Lakeisha said with a groan, muffling a yawn behind her hand. ''I, for one, am thoroughly exhausted.''

Julia's stomach swirled at the casual mention of Zeke's name. She'd heard him clumping around upstairs and wondered what he was doing. She almost wished she *had* chosen kitchen duty. Diapers were the ultimate in monotony.

Lakeisha yawned again, as if to prove Julia's point. ''This day hasn't been so bad,'' Julia said, voicing her thoughts.

Lakeisha laughed. ''You thought it would be bad?''

''Awful,'' Julia admitted. ''Who wants to spend the day cleaning?''

It was for Evy, and she'd thrown herself with a vengeance into washing, drying and folding the huge piles of laundry, and it had helped her work off some of the anger, confusion and other emotions swirling inside her. She felt like a bottle of carbonated soda pop that had been thoroughly shaken and was ready to explode the moment someone twisted the lid.

''Anyone for a hamburger?'' called a booming bass down the stairwell.

Julia and Lakeisha took one look at each other and dashed for the stairs, each trying to be the first to reach the kitchen. The one issue the roommates consistently agreed on was food—and hamburgers topped the list for both of them.

"I'm starving," Lakeisha said, reaching the landing first. "It's about time you fed us poor, work-worn souls, you big lug."

"Hey!" Julia exclaimed, pointing to the telltale bags littering the kitchen table. "These hamburgers are take-out!"

Zeke grinned sheepishly and shrugged. "I was tired of cooking."

"Cheater," Lakeisha admonished, reaching for a burger.

"I'm appalled, Zeke. I thought at the very least we were going to have an opportunity to sample your fine gourmet cuisine. Instead, we get take-out. I'm sooo disappointed." Julia ended her sentence on a sigh.

"We should boycott him," Lakeisha suggested. "Eat at a separate table."

Zeke frowned dramatically. "And I thought I was getting you a special treat," he said with a shrug. "Oh, well. I guess I'll just have to drink all these chocolate milkshakes by myself. Seems a shame."

Julia immediately moved to his side, teasingly curling an arm around his waist. He didn't appear to mind.

"Did someone say chocolate milkshakes?" she purred. Stretching on tiptoe, Julia reached to peek into the bag Zeke held, but he only grinned and lifted it higher, above her reach.

"Ah, ah," he teased. "I'm not sure you *deserve* a milkshake."

"Sorry, Lakeisha, but I'm changing allegiances," Julia declared, still reaching for the bag Zeke held teasingly over his head.

"Concede?" he asked in an equally husky tone, his intention clear.

Julia felt her cheeks warm as Zeke pinned her with his gaze. She knew Lakeisha was watching every action, and was no doubt amused by the scene. Zeke stood motionless, the bag over his head like a mistletoe offering, amusement glowing from his eyes.

Her heart hammered, even as her mind told her this was just a ridiculous, flirtatious game and nothing more.

But it didn't feel like a game as she stood on tiptoe, pulling on Zeke's flannel collar to get his face on her level. The sweet, alluring scent of sawdust brushed her nostrils, and she could feel his heart beating under her palm.

Taking a deep breath, she closed her eyes and brushed her lips across the coarse roughness of his cheek just above the line of his beard.

Lakeisha applauded, Zeke chuckled and Julia blushed to the roots of her hair.

"Chocolate milkshake," she reminded the grinning man with his arm still half around her.

"A woman after my own heart," he teased. He lowered the bag and presented each lady with their prize dessert.

"How are things in the world of laundry?" Zeke queried lightly.

"We're never going to get done," Julia groused. "I had no idea one baby could have so many items of clothing. Not to mention diapers."

"I'm finished up here," Zeke said just before he took a bite of his hamburger. "I mean, everything is prepared and most of it is in the oven. I just have to keep track of the time so I can finish baking the other dishes."

Lakeisha's black eyebrows shot up under the line of her wiry bangs. "You're joking, right?"

Zeke's grin was all male, that *man conquers world* look that sent such tremors through Julia's heart. She laughed heartily.

Lakeisha switched her gaze to Julia, and Julia didn't like the gleam she saw in her roommate's eyes. It meant trouble, the kind with a capital *T*.

"What?" she queried softly, knowing she didn't want to know.

"Well, it just occurred to me," Lakeisha said with a light gesture of her hand, "that I have some things I need to do at home. I have some important paperwork I need to finish. And I think I need to clean my room,'' she added for good measure.

Julia knew full well Lakeisha's room was spotless, as was their whole house. Lakeisha was an obsessive housecleaner. ''What are you doing?'' she whispered frantically.

Lakeisha winked at her roommate. ''You'll see.''

Zeke, who'd been unable to comment due to the hamburger he was chewing, swallowed and spoke up. ''You know, Lakeisha, since I'm done with the cooking, I can help Julia finish up, and you can go ahead and leave.''

Lakeisha's grin amplified by a million watts. ''Are you sure? That would be fantastic.''

''No problem,'' Zeke agreed with a nod. ''We'll be fine here by ourselves.''

She turned her shining gaze on Julia. ''That, my dear roommate, is what I was *doing*. Enjoy.''

Before Julia could so much as swat at Lakeisha for completely humiliating her, Lakeisha was out the door and revving the engine on her car.

So much had gone on the last few weeks, and so many emotions whirled through her, that she was almost afraid to turn around and face Zeke. He was a good man. She didn't know what to do with him, how to categorize him in her mind and heart.

In short, he frightened her.

But when she turned and her gaze met Zeke's, a

dash of hope sprinkled over her. Hope driven by the cool, calm strength and steadfast faith reflected in the pools of his huge blue eyes.

Hope.

She clung to that feeling. With her world going haywire, and her father trying to steal his way back into her life, practically stalking her like a criminal, she needed all the hope she could get.

Chapter Ten

"Did I hear a touch of worry back there, Julia?" Zeke queried gently. He'd moved to stand directly behind her. His breath lightly fanned her hair, and his hands lightly spanned her waist.

She whirled to face him, not sure to be angered or relieved that he had noticed. His gaze met hers in a compassionate, unwavering gaze.

"I guess so," Julia admitted, exhaling sharply. "My father being in town is stressing me out." She hadn't voiced that thought before, and it frightened her. "Not much I can do about it, though."

Zeke stroked her cheek with the backs of his fingers. His hand felt rough against her skin, yet oddly reassuring. She wanted to reach up and press his hand there, holding the moment, but it was only a thought, and one she would never act upon.

"Sometimes it's tough dealing with past feelings and issues, especially with loved ones. With family."

Moving away from her and giving her much needed space, he turned one of the kitchen chairs around and straddled it, resting his chin on his thick forearms.

"You sound as if you speak from experience," Julia said, following his example and seating herself at the table, albeit forward on her chair.

"I do." He didn't elaborate.

Julia was on the verge of asking him what he meant, when they were interrupted by a loud whirring sound, which punctuated itself from time to time with thumps that sounded much like metal on metal.

Their gazes met, and her eyes widened in surprise.

"What do you think?" Zeke asked, his voice low and his lips hiding a smile.

Julia laughed, and they both raced for the stairs, jostling each other in their haste to be the first to the basement.

It was immediately evident that the washing machine was the originator of the terrible sounds. With every turn it knocked from side to side. Smoke and sparks rose from the rear of the machine. Soapy lather spouted in rhythm from the interior and splattered all over the floor, popping up the lid as if the machine had taken on a life of its own.

Julia turned to Zeke, waiting for his response, but he simply stood with his arms crossed over his massive chest, literally gaping at the spewing appliance, his blue eyes shining with amusement.

"Aren't you going to do something?" Julia demanded, grasping a handful of blue flannel on his sleeve and shaking his arm.

"Huh?" It was the first time she'd ever seen him look apprehensive. Stunned, even.

"What is it you want me to do?"

"I don't know! You're the carpenter."

"Precisely," he agreed hastily. "I work with wood. I don't know the first thing about electrical appliances."

"Men!" Julia exclaimed with an aggravated howl. She stomped toward the machine and pulled at the timer handle.

Nothing happened.

She pulled again, and the knob came off in her hand. The machine continued to rumble and sputter, unscathed by her advances.

"Terrific," she protested loudly over the noise of the machine. "Now what?"

She waved the knob at Zeke, almost shaking it at him. "*Do* something!"

His only move was in his expression, as he lifted his eyebrows in question. "What exactly would you suggest?"

"This thing is going to set the house on fire if you don't hurry."

Zeke was amused. So much for the battle of the sexes.

The washing machine was broken. And she expected him to fix it. Never mind that he didn't know anything more than she did about washing machines.

Less, perhaps. He mimicked the tenor of his thoughts, screwing one eye closed and biting on his lower lip in an imitation of Popeye.

The most ironic, hilarious part of the process was that he knew what to do with the machine. He'd known all along.

But he liked to watch Julia with her feathers ruffled. She was adorable. She made his heart catch in his throat.

But she did have a point. The dragonlike, soap-spewing washing machine needed to be conquered, and he, apparently, was the knight errant in shining armor who could perform the noble task.

With one quick sweep, he leaned over, wrapped his hand around the cord, and deftly unplugged the machine from the wall.

Instantly the spewing and flaming ceased, leaving in its wake only the quiet fizz of popping soap bubbles.

"Your dragon is slain, fair lady," he teased.

Julia pinched her lips together, and Zeke thought

she might be angry with herself for not having thought of the wall plug. She was definitely a Type A woman, always needing to be in control of everything.

He'd probably done her a service. Given her the opportunity to see her own inadequacies. He chuckled aloud at the wry thought.

"What are you laughing at?" she demanded, and then pointed at her feet. "Did you happen to notice that our feet are covered in soapy water?

Surprised, Zeke followed the direction of her gesture and suddenly realized they really were standing ankle-deep in soapsuds.

He hadn't even noticed. His work boots kept out the moisture, but surely he should have been aware he was slapping around in the water when he moved.

Julia looked as if she might laugh, scream, or even cry, and all of the sudden their situation didn't seem so funny.

Or maybe it was. He just had to convince Julia to see the absurdity of the situation.

"Submerged sneakers," he commented wryly, letting his amusement show on his face. "Well, at least we don't have to worry about burning the house down."

Julia gave a shaky chuckle, and then put a hand to her throat and began to laugh in earnest. "Only getting electrocuted."

Arms akimbo and hips cocked to one side, she pasted Zeke with a saucy look that made him stop breathing, then tilted her chin and asked, ''How come you couldn't fix that machine?''

Zeke copied her movements. He placed his hands on his hips and said in his best falsetto voice, and in an exact replica of the tone she had used, ''How come you thought I *could* fix that machine?''

''I don't know,'' she said, sounding defensive.

Zeke shifted his posture, wondering how to deal with a woman whose moods shifted faster than the Colorado weather.

Julia removed her hands from her hips and crossed them over her chest. ''My father could have fixed it.''

Zeke bristled. ''Oh, I see.''

Again, he followed her movements, amplifying the motion as he crossed his arms over his chest. ''So I don't measure up to Daddy's standards, do I?''

''I thought...'' She stammered to a halt, then tried again. ''Daddy—my *father*—is a jack-of-all-trades.''

''Who knows how to fix washing machines,'' he finished for her.

''Well, y-yes,'' she stammered.

''You've discovered my weakness,'' he joked with a shrug. ''I am helpless before fire-breathing electrical appliances.''

So much for a knight in shining armor. He relegated himself to squire in her eyes.

"You did all right with this one," she argued softly, patting the now quiet machine. "See? He's not even breathing smoke anymore."

Zeke tried to smile, but it came out as a half grin pinched on one side of his face. "I'm an expert builder, and I can cook a gourmet meal, but I'm completely useless in the electrical department."

"Where'd you learn how to cook?" Julia asked, sounding genuine and friendly, and obviously trying to lure him into a more cheerful subject.

Brimming with genuine and distinctively feminine compassion and sincerity, this was the Julia that Zeke knew.

And loved.

He cleared his throat rapidly, forcing his mind to answer her question, to dwell on facts and not feelings. "I learned to cook in a soup kitchen, believe it or not. I work downtown in one of the homeless shelters on Tuesday nights. They wanted me to cook. Once I discovered I had a knack for it, I started experimenting with gourmet cooking on my own. Following along with those television guys, you know?"

He grunted and shook his head. "I never thought about it before, but I suppose gourmet cooking is a pretty strange hobby for a carpenter, huh?"

She immediately made a sound of denial in her

throat and waved him off with her hand, swishing it through the blond hair cascading down her shoulders.

Zeke swallowed hard. It was hard to focus sometimes. Julia's inner and outer beauty sometimes struck him hard, right between the eyes.

Like right now. He labored to catch a breath.

"I'm jealous," she admitted softly. "I can't cook a single thing. Not to save my life."

He winked. "I'll have you over some night and give you cooking lessons."

As soon as the words were out of his mouth, he realized how awful they sounded. Like he was coming onto her or something. He cringed inwardly, desperately wanting to take the words back.

Unfortunately, there was no way to eat his words and regain the camaraderie they'd previously shared.

Afraid to look at her, but needing to express his remorse, he slowly turned his gaze to her.

She surprised him, taking his words at face value, as they'd been meant. "I'd like that, Zeke," she agreed softly, then smiled and reached for his arm, a brief, soft touch that did more to reassure him than a thousand words would have done. "In the meantime, though, I'd like to hear more of what you do at the soup kitchen."

"I'm happy to tell you, Julia," he said, more earnestly than she'd ever know.

She laughed; a light, ringing sound that delighted his ears and made him want to laugh, too.

"No time like the present. But I think we better talk over a couple of mops. What do you think?" She winked at him.

What he thought was that his heart had stopped dead in his chest, but outwardly he kept moving, as if he weren't walking a figurative foot off the ground.

He found two worn sponge mops and a bucket in the utility closet. He handed a mop to Julia and kept one for himself. He tried to place the plastic bucket on the floor, but it floated, so he placed it on the now silently contrite washer.

"We'd better get busy if we want to have this mess cleaned up by Christmas."

With Christmas only three weeks away, Zeke wasn't being overly sarcastic, Julia thought wryly. She applied herself to her mop, vigorously plying and squeezing dirty, soapy water into the bucket, which one of the two of them dumped into the sink on a regular basis.

As they mopped, Zeke told her of the homeless men and women he'd met, and how hungry they were, not only for food, but also for an answer to their problems.

Julia hurt for them, even as she heard about them. She wanted to be like Zeke. She wanted to help the homeless, just as she wanted to help women in crisis pregnancies. There were so many needs, and she felt for them all.

She wanted to help everyone.

The knowledge that she wasn't capable of such philanthropy was part of what had given birth to her now defunct *Great Scheme.* Marry a pastor. Help all kinds of people. Work right on the front lines.

A little like what Zeke was doing.

The thought surprised her, and she filed it away to reflect on later. ''Tell me more,'' she urged.

''Seeing the little children at the shelters is the hardest part,'' Zeke said, squeezing his mop into the bucket. ''Can you imagine being a homeless, abandoned mother with nowhere to shelter your baby? The little ones...'' He stopped short.

Julia's heart swelled until her chin felt taut with emotion. ''Could I go with you to the homeless shelter sometime?''

Zeke stopped mopping and looked at her full in the face. ''I'd like that,'' he whispered huskily.

Their gazes met and held, and Julia read a symphony of emotions in Zeke's warm blue eyes.

Quite suddenly he broke his gaze away, scooping up the full bucket and dumping the water into the sink. ''What are you doing for Christmas this year?'' he asked with a casual smile.

That smile had her heart dancing a tango across her chest. She was alarmed by the strength of the feelings that passed between them. She wasn't certain she wanted to analyze the thoughts in her head and the emotions running through her heart.

Sometimes it was better not to think too much. This was one of those times. She turned her attention to her mop and the hopelessly wet floor.

"Lakeisha and I always spend Christmas together," she said softly. "We haven't bought a Christmas tree yet, though. We get a small tree—something less than four feet tall. The little ones fit better in our small apartment. But I always get a real tree, not one of those fake jobbies. I love the smell of fresh pine, don't you?"

Zeke apparently chose to ignore her babbling, and honed in on her first sentence. "No family?"

"Nope." Julia frowned, a storm once again brewing. "Well, not anyone I'd care to spend Christmas with, in any case."

Zeke stopped mopping and turned to her, his eyebrows raised in question.

"You're wondering why I don't spend the holidays with my father," she said dully, knowing it was a statement and not a question.

Zeke nodded and leaned his palms onto the top of the mop handle.

Julia hadn't told anyone about her father, except for Lakeisha, and even then, she'd kept her explanations minimal. Lakeisha had seen. She knew. But Julia had never talked about it. The need to share the entire story with someone suddenly seemed too overwhelming a burden to bear. Zeke's compassion, the quiet way he reached out to her, seemed to be the freedom she'd been looking for.

The words poured out of her mouth as quickly as the tears poured down her cheeks.

"I feel kind of foolish," she said, quietly dabbing at her cheeks with the corner of her sweatshirt.

Zeke chuckled softly at her action and handed her his handkerchief from the back pocket of his jeans. His hands easily spanned her waist as he propped her up onto the washing machine, where they'd be face-to-face as she spoke.

"It's not like my story is unique or unusual in this day and age," she protested.

Zeke leaned in on her, one hand on either side of her hips, until his nose was inches from her own and he had her gaze tightly locked with his. His warm breath was the cool sensation of polar ice.

That frightening thought made her try to pull away from him, but he wouldn't let her go. His arms were like steel bands beside her. He wasn't technically even touching her, but she had nowhere to wiggle away from his grasp.

"The issue isn't whether or not your relationship with your father is unique or unusual, Julia. It's *your* story."

The way he said it, combined with the firm, gentle look in his eyes, broke down her reserves. "Okay, but you'll probably be sorry you asked."

"Let me be the judge of that," he said gently, tipping her on the end of the nose with his finger.

"Okay. Well, let's see...my mom and dad married after they'd known each other two weeks."

"It sounds like you should start this story with 'Once upon a time.'"

Julia made a sound that was half a surprised laugh, half a snort. "Doesn't it, though? It gets worse."

Zeke made a sweeping gesture with his arm.

"They met at a country club. She was a debutante, and he a waiter. He swept my mother right off her feet with his charm and good looks. I'm sure teenage rebellion played into it, too. I was never allowed to meet my maternal grandparents, so I couldn't say. My mother tried time and again to mend fences, but my grandparents never reneged."

"Poor little rich girl makes good with the waiter of the country club," he said thoughtfully. "But he married her, so he must have thought he loved her."

"Oh, I'm sure," she agreed, knowing Zeke could hear the derision in her voice. "In fact, I'd wager he'd still say he loves her, if he was questioned on the subject. Carrying a banner for her all the years she's been gone. It's probably what he's come here to try to tell me, not that I'm going to stay around long enough to listen to him."

Zeke frowned. "Then why—"

"Do I detest the man so much?"

''If he loved your mother—''

''You know, that's just it. Everyone around here, you and Lakeisha included, seem to think that if you have love in your relationship, everything else just falls into place.''

Zeke opened his mouth, but Julia held him off, extending her hand palm out.

''I'm here to tell you, it isn't so.''

From the way Zeke's eyebrows hovered low over his eyes, Julia thought he looked ready to argue, but when he didn't open his mouth, she continued. ''My father *loved* my mom, but he couldn't keep a job to save his life. My mom might as well have been a single mother, for all the help he gave her. He'd keep a job for two weeks, sometimes three. And then he'd disappear.''

''Disappear as in completely?'' Zeke asked, sounding genuinely amazed.

''Disappear as in until his money ran completely out,'' Julia modified. ''Then he'd show up again, walk in the door as if nothing had changed.''

''And your mother?''

''My mother never said a word. Not once. At least not in my hearing. I refuse to believe she never chewed him out in private.

''Mom was a Christian, and I believe it was her faith that got her through. She went to counseling, I know. She'd run off without a penny to her name, so she hadn't attended college and couldn't now, with a little girl to support."

Julia's eyes got misty in remembrance of the striking, golden-haired angel whose green eyes were always watching over her. "She left me with the neighbors at night and stocked shelves at a discount store. She was always there for me when I was awake. I think the only sleep she caught was when I was in school."

"Wow," said Zeke, with a low whistle. "She was very dedicated to you, Julia."

"Yes, she was," she said fiercely. "And she saved every penny she earned so I could go to college and get a good education."

"And here you are."

"And here I am. But my mom worked herself into the grave getting me here, so what difference does it make?"

She tore her gaze away from him, looking anywhere but into his warm, compassionate eyes. She didn't need or want sympathy for her situation. She just wanted a better deal for her own kids.

"So why is your father here now, do you think?" Zeke didn't force her to look at him, but the long, comforting strokes of his hand on her hair reminded her all too strongly that he was here. And that he cared.

"I couldn't tell you." She snapped out the words, feeling like she wanted to throw something. "And to tell you the truth, I don't want to know. He left the day my mother was buried six years ago, and he never looked back. I'll tell you one thing—I have nothing to say to him.''

Zeke nodded and shifted his weight to his heels, leaning his thick shoulders against the bare, crusty drywall with no quandary about the dust settling onto his shoulders, making white streaks on his blue flannel. She recognized he was thoughtfully giving her the space she needed.

Julia slipped off the washer and looked at her sopping sneakers, trying to focus on the discomfort of her wet feet rather than the furious squeezing of her heart and throat. She picked at a piece of imaginary lint from the sleeve of her purple sweatshirt. She studied her pinched fingers as if she'd find an answer there.

Zeke moved to her side and took her gently in his arms, stroking her hair and murmuring softly under his breath.

For the first time since her mother's death, Julia allowed herself to cry. Sobs gushed forth, wave after wave in pounding fury.

Zeke's flannel was soon soaked, but he didn't seem to notice. He simply held her, tightly yet gently, and let her vent, until finally, there were no more tears.

Julia was amazed at how she felt. Talking about her childhood had been surprisingly good therapy for her, but finding within her heart the ability to cry—well, Zeke had given her a gift, something she'd never be able to repay.

She sniffled, focusing on regaining her composure.

"Sorry," she apologized at last, her voice cracking. "I got your shirt all wet."

Zeke smiled tenderly. "I don't mind."

He pulled away from her, pausing only to run a finger down her nose, slowly over her lips, to the line of her chin.

Then, suddenly, he backed away, hefting his mop and returning to his job. "I think I can finish up here by myself. There isn't much to do besides mop this mess up. I can't do anything about the washer today. I'll have to call someone to come out and fix it. Why don't you go pick up that Christmas tree you've been talking about and surprise Lakeisha with it."

Julia smiled and thanked him. It wasn't every day you made a friend like Zeke Taylor. But thank God she had.

Chapter Eleven

Even without a family to celebrate with, Julia loved the Christmas season. Peace on earth and goodwill toward men. The snow-covered Rocky Mountains glistening like diamonds in the Colorado sunshine.

Snowmen.

Children laughing.

The sluicing of ice skates as they cut across a frozen pond. Carolers strolling down the Sixteenth Street Mall, their tunes warming the crisp evening air. Christmas shopping at Larimer Square.

The crackle of a winter's fire warming her woolen-sock clad feet as she toasted a marshmallow to a crispy dark brown.

So many happy childhood memories, blissful days full of baking cookies and wrapping presents she'd made especially for her mother. Sometimes she even saved enough change to buy something small and delicate for her small and delicate mother.

Julia whistled a Christmas hymn as she wrapped tiny flickering lights around the lovely little pine she'd purchased at a lot on the way home from the Martins' house.

She inhaled the crisp, lingering scent of fresh pine needles and stepped back to survey her work.

The colored lights twinkled merrily against the deep-green background. The tree tipped to one side about six inches from the top, so the shimmering angel she'd placed there was likewise tilted.

But Julia didn't mind the flaws. Flaws gave a tree character, separating it from its artificial counterparts. Again she inhaled deeply, planning the execution of the numerous decorations ladening the boxes piled around the usually immaculate living room.

First, she decided, she'd pop some corn to string. Then she'd tie Victorian ribbons into fancy bows around some of the branches. After that, she'd garnish the whole thing with a multitude of icicles that would reflect the twinkling lights.

As she strung pieces of popcorn through a long string of thread, she allowed herself to ponder recent events. She immediately recalled the tender look in Zeke's eyes as she'd related her story, the way the two of them connected without words.

He listened without judging her, even when she

herself knew she deserved judgment. Never in her life had she opened herself up to someone the way she had to Zeke. It seemed natural to reveal her true heart.

She *trusted* him.

He was the kind of man a woman could depend on. He had an inner strength that matched his outer might, and he wasn't afraid to share that intensity with others.

But he's not the right man for you, Julia reminded herself.

Money would always be an issue. And she knew firsthand how big an issue money could be in a marriage. Zeke was a hands-on man. What if he got hurt or killed on the job? What if they had to move around a lot so he could find work?

Still, it was getting harder and harder to convince herself there wasn't something between them.

The truth was, she was terrified of the possibilities Zeke brought to light.

She plunged the needle through a piece of popcorn and straight into her finger. She watched silently as a tiny dot of blood pooled where she'd poked herself. The finger began to throb, and she fought the urge to thrust it into her mouth, as a small child would have done.

As the cool water of the kitchen sink bathed her sore extremity, she considered where her own work had brought her. Heartless. Calculated and presumptuous.

She'd chosen Bryan so she wouldn't get hurt the way her mother had been hurt, by falling in love with an imperfect man. She was only now beginning to understand that all men were imperfect, in one way or another.

She'd have to revisit her Scheme with new eyes.

With Zeke she was too vulnerable. She couldn't keep secrets from him. He knew instinctively what she was thinking and feeling. And she certainly wasn't comfortable with the feelings he aroused in her heart. Just thinking about them made her want to panic, to bolt and run.

Bryan was safe. Boring, perhaps; but safe. Besides, he was a pastor.

He was also an egotistical, self-centered piece of work.

She'd never been more confused in her life. She supposed she could scrap the whole thing and start over. Bryan wasn't the only young, single pastor in the world. But the thought of starting over only made her stomach turn. Everything she thought she was, wasn't, and all that wasn't suddenly shone with such potential she could hardly bear to think about it.

As she dried her hands, someone heavily thumped on the front door, waiting no more than three seconds before thumping again. Repeatedly.

Not today, Julia thought, her whole body tensing. *Please, God, no bad surprises today.*

Bryan stood in the corridor, awkwardly attempting to hide a large pot of poinsettias behind his back. A thin smile lined his usually serious face.

"What lousy weather," he announced as she opened the door and ushered him in.

"Come in, Bryan," she said, nearly rolling her eyes at his negative mood and trying not to stare at the profusion of red petals peeking from behind his back.

Father Bryan Cummings catapulted into the room, his face in its usual eagle scowl, the front lock of his fine black hair dividing his face. "Julia, I've got to talk to you about something.

"Are you by yourself? I need to see you *alone* for a few minutes," Bryan announced without preamble. He set the plant he'd been holding aside, as if forgetting he'd even brought it. "It's important, or I wouldn't ask."

As if he had—*asked,* that is. She supposed she should be shocked by his abruptness, but the awful truth was that she expected him to act just the way he had.

How had she ever conceived such a silly notion as to want to ally herself with Bryan? It was a question, she realized, that she should have asked herself months ago. It gave her a chill to realize that in her zeal to find someone she could join in ministry, she'd overlooked one very important point.

Character.

Reluctantly, she turned her attention to Bryan, willing herself to continue her charade; which, she now knew, was exactly what it was. *All* it was.

Bryan's scowl lessened as he pulled up a stool next to her. "Julia," he began, "I have something very important to ask you. I'm sorry it took so long for me to get here to see you. I was busy with the Lord's work, you know."

"Of course," she conceded, though she wondered what *Lord's work* would keep him from visiting a friend. She refrained from asking, and Bryan didn't elaborate.

"I don't know that you've noticed, Julia," he said, punctuating her name, "but you and I work well together in ministry."

Julia nodded, tapping her fingernails on the countertop. This was some kind of cockeyed dream turned into a nightmare. It couldn't be happening.

"Well, I think it's time we became partners in the Lord."

Julia, trying to sip at her water glass, gagged and sputtered. Water went down the wrong pipe, and she swallowed hard, gasping for air. The pain and burning probably served her right, she thought grimly.

She coughed several more times before she could speak. "Come again?"

When he smiled, his lips looked out of place with the rest of his dark features.

"My graduation from seminary is coming up in May." He smiled grandly. "I'm planning to start a new evangelistic ministry—the Bryan Cummings Evangelistic Ministries."

He let that sink in a moment before continuing. "I'm going to travel all over the country, and of course internationally. I'm going to speak to huge crowds of lost and unsaved people, and win thousands of souls to the Lord. Can you see it, Julia? Can you catch my vision here?"

Why stop at thousands, she wanted to ask, obstinately desiring to stick a pin into his inflated ego; but she reluctantly stifled the childish ambition, and attempted to quell her stirring anger.

"I'm going to need an advertising and publicity executive, and of course I immediately thought of you. You're perfect for the job."

The advertising and publicity manager for an international evangelistic ministry.

It was a tempting offer, the kind of step up in her career that she'd been searching for. She had no doubt Father Bryan would be a huge success in his effort. He was wholly devoted to his career, and he had the Midas touch in everything he tried. If his stories were anything to go by, he'd been starting and operating successful ministries since high school. She could ride the wave of ministry with him—help who knew how many thousands of people every year.

It was certainly the opportunity to help people on a much broader scope than she was operating on now. Her internal paintbrush was already painting the colorful canvass for her.

Wasn't that what she wanted?

She felt as if her lungs were ready to explode. All her goals, dreams and desires—nearly everything she'd been working for and dreaming about, were being handed to her on a silver platter.

She was being given the opportunity to be a part of something bigger than herself. To be in a position where she could really count. To use her God-given gifts to work in a *big* way for the cause of Christ, instead of the small, life-by-life ministry she was experiencing now.

Her thoughts slammed to a halt like a freight train on brakes.

Her goals—and her dreams—had *changed,* she realized with a start. She didn't know what the future held, but she suddenly knew in her heart, with the kind of peaceful assurance that only comes from God, that her future—and her heart—weren't in touring the world with Father Bryan Cummings.

"You don't have to answer right away," Bryan assured her. "I know this is going to be a big move for you, from a small, local agency to a worldwide ministry. But don't worry. I think you're up to it."

"Actually, I'm not," she retorted, more than a little offended by his patronizing tone.

"What?"

"Your offer—the position—sounds wonderful, and I'm honored that you thought of me. But I'm afraid I'm going to have to decline. I don't think working for you is God's best for me right now. I'm sorry."

She was thinking about the local soup kitchen, and the women at HeartBeat—the young teens and frightened wives. A person didn't have to be great in order to touch lives.

Only big. Bighearted, like Zeke.

Father Bryan looked dumbstruck. "You don't want to pray about it first?"

"I don't believe my answer would change, Bryan. God is taking me in a different direction right now, and I've got to follow His lead."

"You're sure?"

"Yes. Absolutely. But again, I appreciate your thinking of me."

"All right, then," Bryan said, abruptly standing and clearing his throat noisily. "I'd better leave now. You know how it is. A pastor's work is never done."

She watched without emotion as he let himself out of the apartment. Maybe it was shock, but she couldn't dismiss the tiny inkling of relief emanating from the general area of her stomach.

There were still many things to work out, but at least she'd pitched her Great Scheme in favor of finding God's way for her. "A man plans his way, but his steps are the Lord's."

Zeke crouched low, his back tight against the cold concrete. Bryan Cummings strode from Julia's apartment and within five feet of Zeke, but the pastor never saw him hunkered there.

Zeke's right hand clenched the bouquet of pink carnations he held on his lap. He wanted to hurl the wretched flowers over the edge of the landing and let them fall heedlessly where they would, but something inside him stopped him from the action.

Father Bryan had beaten him to the punch. Zeke had no sooner exited his truck, than he'd seen Bryan striding purposefully up the walk, a large pot of poinsettias in his hand.

Zeke knew exactly where he was going, and he could guess why. And that *why* made his carnations insignificant.

Pink carnations, for crying out loud. Why hadn't he been more romantic, more thoughtful?

Poinsettias? Julia would love those. And Bryan had known.

Zeke had merely wanted to buy Julia something as an expression of their growing friendship, and perhaps as a hint of his own growing feelings for her.

Not roses, the clerk at the flower shop had said. Not unless you mean love.

He did, but he didn't want to be pushy. With what Julia had told him about her past, the last thing he wanted to do was appear too forceful.

Now he wouldn't appear anything at all.

What was he thinking? That he could win the love and devotion of the kindest, sweetest woman he'd ever known?

If only love were so easy.

Chapter Twelve

"Does Lakeisha need a ride?" Zeke asked as he gave Julia a lift into his truck. Julia hadn't seen him in a week, and was surprised how much she'd missed him.

"No," she responded with a laugh. "Lakeisha sleeps until the last possible moment, then cranks it in gear all the way to church. We'll see her there without a moment to spare."

"Hopefully not with a speeding ticket in her hand," Zeke joked under his breath.

She slipped a glance at him, her straight-toothed smile so clear and bright that his breath caught in his throat.

"That's why I called you for a ride when I knew my car was going to be in the shop this weekend. I needed someone dependable."

Zeke tensed, squeezing the steering wheel with both fists. *Good old dependable Zeke.* Was that all he'd ever be to her?

And yet, she had phoned *him,* out of all her friends and acquaintances, for this little favor. Did he dare read anything into the action?

When they arrived at the church, Julia indicated her usual preference of the second pew from the front. Zeke suspected it had something to do with being close to Bryan, who always helped serve the Eucharist.

He hoped he was wrong.

Zeke mentally shook his head, extremely annoyed with himself. Here he was in the sanctuary at church, and his mind was on the potential situation between Bryan and Julia. He knew he should quiet his roaring mind and focus on worshipping God.

He fidgeted in his seat and slid to his knees, hoping prayer would set his mind on things above. But as he glanced to his right where Julia sat, he knew it was beyond him to do. He prayed God would forgive him for it. After all, He had made Julia in the first place. And He must know He'd made her irresistible to this simple carpenter.

There was one sure way to put himself out of his misery, he realized as he slid back to his seat on the pew next to her.

He could ask her out. On a real date.

He stretched his arms out on either side of him

as he lounged back in the pew, his Rockies baseball cap clasped in one fist. He was suddenly aware of his clothing, his red flannel shirt, fastened at the neck with a black cotton tie that felt way too tight all of a sudden.

He cleared his throat and pressed his hand upon Julia's shoulder, a casual attempt to get her attention.

She quickly turned her smile upon Zeke, and his words froze on his tongue.

It only took a moment, but a moment was enough.

Father Bryan slid into the pew in front of Julia and leaned toward her, his gaze quickly capturing hers. Zeke knew Bryan would have no trouble with his words.

Father Bryan looked as formidable as always in black clericals and his trademark scowl firmly in place.

But Bryan didn't speak. He only looked at Julia for a moment, then stood and cleared his throat, a clear prelude to a speech.

"I've got an important announcement to make after the service today," he said, loud enough for everyone around them to hear.

Bryan slid Julia a knowing look in the process. He tilted his chin in the air in what Zeke thought was a high-hat manner, even for Father Bryan.

Julia broke eye contact and looked away, and Bryan's scowl deepened. With a loud huff of breath, he turned and stalked away without explaining what his wordless conversation was all about.

Zeke knew now wasn't the time to press the issue of wanting to be near Julia, but he still found it hard to concentrate. He had much to be thankful for, and the familiar liturgy of the service drew him in.

Even so, by the end of the service, his heart had migrated to the right of him, where Julia sat. He was bursting to ask her out, to make his feelings official, and found it practically unbearable to have to sit quietly in the pew.

Immediately following the benediction, and with a hearty *Thanks be to God,* Zeke reached for Julia's hand, determined to make this day the day things changed—before he lost the courage to do so.

"Excuse me, everyone." Bryan moved to the pulpit and spoke into the microphone attached to his alb. "Will you please remain seated for just one moment? I've got an important announcement to make."

Zeke heaved a sigh of impatience, feeling almost as if Bryan was purposefully throwing stumbling stones at his feet.

Bryan leaned into the pulpit, peering into the congregation until he was certain he had everyone's undivided attention. Then, maximizing his propensity for drama, he stepped out from behind the right pulpit and walked to the middle of the aisle.

"This is a very happy day for me," he said without flavor. "I would like you all to share my joy."

Zeke choked. Was he announcing an engagement?

To Julia?

He slid a glance in her direction, but she was rustling through her purse. He couldn't see the expression her face.

Bryan's next words gave him a temporary reprieve. "This week, I incorporated the name Bryan Cummings Evangelistic Ministries."

Zeke let out the breath he'd been holding. Everyone applauded politely, and Bryan basked in the glow for as long as he could milk it.

Lakeisha, who'd appeared out of nowhere at the end of the service and had slid into the pew next to Julia, squeezed Julia's hand.

"This is it," she whispered loud enough for Zeke to hear. She sounded excited, and Zeke couldn't help but be curious about the meaning of her words.

He didn't have long to wait.

Bryan's smooth tenor voice eased through the sanctuary. "My ministry stands to make a great difference in the world, winning many thousands of men and women to Christ, both here in America and internationally. We'll be headquartered in Palm Beach, Florida, so I'll be leaving Grace Church and HeartBeat at the end of this term."

Again, he waited for the stir to die down.

"Today, I'd like to publicly ask a particular woman, someone right here in this congregation, to join my team. I want her to be the first to say she'll relocate to Florida to help serve the Lord at BCEM."

Julia.

Zeke didn't wait around to hear the words said aloud. He rolled from his seat and stalked from the sanctuary as fast as he could, not caring if people wondered at his action.

Not caring.

Please, God, not caring.

Julia was convinced no one could miss the way Bryan pierced her directly with his sharp stare. If she could have turned herself into liquid and drained through the floorboards, she would have gladly done so. A gigantic porcupine was rolling around in her stomach, sending pins and needles of pain into every extremity.

That her plans concerning Bryan could have come to such an implausible conclusion, and with such dreadful timing, was unthinkable.

Thank the Lord she'd come to her senses before she'd set off on a wild-goose chase called Bryan Cummings Evangelistic Ministries. Serving dinner at a soup kitchen was much more to her liking, especially with Zeke by her side.

And she would be working for the *right* reasons

this time—because she loved God and *wanted* to help others, not because it was some kind of spiritual requirement she had to meet.

She realized Bryan was staring at her, and she lifted both eyebrows, wondering what he was waiting for. Was he expecting some kind of reaction from her? To stand and be recognized?

The effects of the moment were far-reaching, she realized, the porcupine turning to a knot deep in her stomach. If Bryan publicly asked her to join his team, she'd have a difficult time turning him down. People would assume she wanted the position. It would be awkward and embarrassing to explain amidst congratulatory wishes, and she was certain that was exactly what Bryan had in mind.

The fact that she'd already turned him down once didn't seem to phase him. He wasn't the type of man to take rejection well.

Evidently, he didn't take rejection at *all.*

Bryan had to know he was forcing her hand.

She sucked in a breath and caught her bottom lip between her teeth. Every nerve vibrated against her skin as she waited for the words that would create an entirely new set of difficulties, and complicate everything in her life a hundredfold.

Lakeisha, evidently sensing and misunderstanding Julia's tension, again squeezed her hand. Lakeisha saw the opportunity here, even if it was Father Bryan making the offering.

She sighed and closed her eyes, unable to look to her left side, where Zeke sat. She could imagine all too well what he must think.

"And so," continued Bryan after another extended pause, "I want you all to congratulate my new Executive Coordinator of Publicity and Advertising, Miss Julia Evans!"

Julia stood to the applause, then took a deep breath and moved to Father Bryan's side. With a wave of her hand, the small conversations around her ceased.

"I am flattered," she said slowly, carefully choosing her words, "by the generosity Father Bryan has shown in selecting me to be one of the key members of his new team at BCEM. I believe this ministry will have a profound impact, and am excited by the direction Father Bryan is taking it."

Her church family applauded warmly, which only served to tighten the knot in Julia's gut.

"While I'm honored," she continued, keeping her voice steady even when her hands were shaking, "I will not be able to accept this position."

Any lingering conversations came to a quick halt, and the sanctuary echoed with silence.

"Bryan's organization appeals to me in many ways, but I believe God would have me stay here in Denver. With HeartBeat. And with you at Grace Church. I'm very committed to the ministry here, and after searching my heart, I truly believe that's where God wants me to stay right now."

To Julia's surprise, there was much supportive applause amidst the confusion and titters of conversation. She didn't blame the congregation for not understanding what was going on.

She blamed Bryan.

It gave her something constructive to do with her mind, figuring out a hundred different ways to torture the man. With a last nod, she smiled shakily and sat down hard on the front pew. She felt as if she'd broken out in a sweat, but knew that was just her imagination working overtime.

People flooded forward, offering Bryan their best wishes. Julia didn't budge an inch from her seat. Zeke had disappeared somewhere. She was certain he believed she would—maybe should—take the position. She wanted him to know she'd be staying around.

But she wasn't moving from this building until she'd had a chance to speak her mind to Father Bryan. He slid her the occasional sidelong glance, perhaps hoping she'd take off and save him the embarrassment.

He could nurse his hope all he wanted. It was possible she'd let him off the hook. It was possible pigs would learn to fly.

Just not very probable, she thought with a tight-lipped smile. Lakeisha asked if she should stay, but

Julia waved her away. This was between two people and only two people, not the entire congregation, as Bryan would have it.

Eventually, the crowd ebbed and Father Bryan loosened his alb and started gathering his things together. Julia waited until everyone had cleared the sanctuary, but then she wasted no time moving to his side.

''What exactly were you trying to pull back there?'' she snapped, though keeping her voice low in the acoustic echo of the church.

Bryan looked straight at her, his brown eyes wide with surprise. ''What would that be?''

She lifted a sardonic eyebrow. ''What do you suppose I'm talking about?'' The man was either obtuse or plain stupid, but Julia doubted either.

Bryan took a deep breath and scowled, his dark eyebrows meeting at a sharp point just above his eaglelike nose. ''Why did you embarrass me like that?''

''Excuse me?''

''I just offered you the best position you'll ever get the chance to take, and you publicly humiliated me in my own church.''

Julia pulled in a deep breath to steady her thundering heart. ''No, Bryan. You've got that wrong. You offered the position to me the other day, and I *turned you down.* How could you have forgotten something that important? Or were you trying to goad me, to force my hand?''

''I was trying to make you see what's good for you,'' Bryan retorted. ''You didn't know what you were saying. You hadn't had time to pray about it.''

''I knew exactly what I was saying,'' Julia assured him blandly.

Bryan whirled on her so quickly she didn't have time to react. She winced as his fingers clamped on to the tender flesh of her upper arms. ''Don't make the biggest mistake of your life, Julia.''

''Oh, I won't,'' Her eyes widened as she realized just how true that statement was.

Bryan's eyes gleamed with excitement. ''Then you'll join me in ministry?''

In his zeal, he was shaking her by the shoulders, though Julia doubted he realized he was even holding on to her. ''No, Bryan. That's not what I meant.''

''But you have to—''

Julia tried to pull from his grasp, but he tightened his grip and pulled her close to his face. ''I have to succeed in this,'' he hissed desperately.

''Let her go.''

Bryan's grip turned into a vise at the command of the deep, imposing voice.

Zeke.

She'd never been happier to see anyone in her

life. She had no idea why he'd returned to the church, but she was definitely glad he was here.

He strode to her side and broke Bryan's grip from her arms in one quick, smooth movement. And then she was safe in Zeke's arms, those tight bands of steel wrapping around her and offering her the support she hadn't even recognized she'd needed.

She started shaking. At the time, she hadn't realized Bryan had actually frightened her, but now, belatedly, she was acutely aware of her heart pounding in her ears.

"If you try to manhandle Julia again," Zeke said through clenched teeth, "I *will* find out about it. And you will answer to me."

Bryan's face drained to a deathly white.

"Do we understand each other?"

Bryan tried to speak, but only stammered unintelligible syllables. He pulled his Bible to his chest like a shield and beelined for the sacristy of the church.

Julia felt rather than heard the deep rumble in Zeke's chest. She wasn't sure if it was a growl or a chuckle, but he was definitely following Bryan's retreat with interest. His heartbeat was regular and familiar, and she clung to him a moment longer, until her pragmatic nature took over and reminded her that she had her face buried in a man's shirt.

His shirt smelled good, too—*he* smelled good. The familiar scent of wood and man that was distinctly Zeke enveloped her every bit as much as his arms did.

He, too, apparently took stock of their situation, for he cleared his throat and stepped away, leaving only one hand on her shoulder for support.

"Are you okay?" he asked gruffly, his fingers softly toying with the hair curling at the nape of her neck.

She shivered, and thought it probably wasn't due to her close call with Bryan.

"I am now," she whispered. He wrapped both arms around her, and she allowed him to pull her back into his embrace. The steady beat of his heart was more welcome than he would ever know. "Now that you're here, everything's fine."

Chapter Thirteen

For several minutes, Julia stood staring at the large red Christmas flowers she'd placed on her mantel, unable to categorize her feelings. With a disgruntled growl, she tossed the innocent flowers into the trash bin by her desk.

Her entire life had turned upside down in a single morning. How was that possible?

Or maybe it had been longer than that. Maybe she'd known what was coming this morning, and had instinctively prepared for the grenade Bryan threw in her direction. Prepared, as in run like crazy and dive for cover.

Sighing audibly, she pulled the rumpled flowers from the bin and placed them back on the mantel. It wasn't the poinsettia's fault men were so difficult.

Easily diverted on this lazy afternoon, she stared

blankly out the window, admiring the frost-covered pines surrounding the apartment complex, when Lakeisha whirled into the apartment, her arms full of shopping bags.

''Hell-o, girlfriend,'' Lakeisha exclaimed with a laugh.

She was a study in animation, her dark cheeks flushed rose from the crisp evening air. She dumped her parcels onto the sofa, grunting from the effort.

''Been shopping, I see,'' Julia said, responding to Lakeisha's light manner in kind, glad of the deep relationship they shared, where sometimes words were not needed at all.

Julia wondered at her friend's apparent happiness, and privately admitted to being more than a little jealous. Lakeisha was a good-natured woman in general, but today she was full to bursting with brilliance and energy.

Julia watched with wry humor as her roommate flopped onto the blue Victorian armchair, wrenching her boots from her feet and tossing them in the general direction of the front closet. She stretched and yawned, her lounging movements reminding Julia of a spoiled exotic kitten.

''Sit with me,'' Lakeisha suggested, pointing at the worn sofa. ''I have news—I won't be here for Christmas.''

Julia felt as if her stomach were doing somersaults. If Lakeisha left, she would be completely and utterly alone over the holidays.

Talk about abandoned...

"Why?" Julia asked softly, although she already knew in her heart.

Lakeisha's eyes brightened, and the slow flush that had begun to recede now reappeared on her dark cheeks. "Girl, I'm so excited! My mom is actually staying home this year, instead of traveling all over the world and back. Christmas in America. What a novel concept."

Julia swallowed hard and bit back tears, but Lakeisha didn't appear to notice her distress.

Her roommate laughed gaily. "You know she's been seeing that Robert Martin guy, the historian? Well, I guess it's getting serious. It was his idea, actually, I think. *They* want me to drive out to Wisconsin to spend the holidays with the both of them, Mom said." She swept in a big, happy breath and encompassed the room with the broad gesture of her arms. "At *home*."

Julia did her best to smile, but knew the effort was absorbed by her protesting heart. Just thinking back to their small, shared hometown in Wisconsin was enough to bring tears to her eyes. She hadn't visited since the day she graduated from high school. "How nice for you."

The words sounded stilted, even to Julia. She was happy for her friend, truly she was. But...

Lakeisha sprung from the armchair like a cat, the rosy flush turning to red splotches. She closed the distance quickly and threw her arms around Julia's shoulders, dancing them both around in circles.

"I think he's going to ask Mom to marry him," she confided joyfully.

Of course. It made perfect sense. Meet the family. Pop the question. In this cockeyed day and age, when a man wanted to meet a woman's daughter...

She felt as if she were losing a sister, even though the rational side of her brain reminded her how silly she was being.

"What's that smell?" Lakeisha asked, changing the subject.

"Smell?" Julia was grateful to her friend for accepting the gesture and changing the subject, but she had no idea what her roommate was talking about.

"Flowers or something." Lakeisha sniffed the air, turning toward the fragrance of the poinsettias. "Where'd you get these?"

"Bryan."

Lakeisha lifted an eyebrow. "Way to go, girl. It isn't a dozen red roses, but it's a great start to that Great Scheme of yours."

"Ugh." Julia cringed. "Please don't remind me that I ever considered marrying a man like Father Bryan."

Lakeisha belted out a laugh, and then jumped as sudden knock startled both of them.

"Who is it?" Lakeisha called.

"Special delivery for Julia Evans."

Lakeisha shrieked merrily. "More flowers for you, Julia, do you think?" she teased, an amused gleam in her eye as she whipped the door open. "Do you think they're from Father Bryan or Zeke?"

Zeke send her flowers?

Shaking her head at her own silliness, she swallowed the lump that had formed in her throat, and moved to the door, wondering why Lakeisha had suddenly grown silent.

Her roommate seldom gave up the tease without nursing it for all it was worth.

"Julia isn't here."

Lakeisha's words startled Julia so that she moved in the direct line of door. "What do you mean I'm not here?"

Before her roommate even had the opportunity to huff out a breath and give her *the* look, Julia knew exactly what she was talking about.

She fervently *wished* herself *not here.*

"Julia, I've come to apologize about the other night," her father said from just outside the door. "I've brought you flowers. Pink carnations, your favorite."

Now how did her on-again off-again father know that private and very personal information? A swift frost gathered at the top of her neck and raced down the tendrils of her back.

Lakeisha hastily threw herself between them. ''Julia has made it crystal clear she doesn't want to speak to you.''

Greg Evans grinned rakishly. ''Call me persistent.''

That was enough to bring a groan from Julia's lips. And enough to help her make her mind up.

When Lakeisha opened her mouth to speak, Julia stepped forward and reached for her hand. ''You've been a great friend in this,'' she said, with a grateful squeeze. ''But I think it's time I had him in and got this over with, don't you?''

Lakeisha's eyebrows disappeared behind her black bangs. ''It's your call, girl.''

Julia shrugged. It was enough to send her skeptical roommate back to her own room, grabbing a muffin on the way.

Greg Evans grinned jauntily at his daughter, then swept his still-blond hair off his face with his palm, and presented the bouquet of pink carnations with a flourish, a small wrapped Christmas gift still tucked under his arm.

''Save it,'' Julia rumbled, before whirling on her heels and tramping back into her living room. If he followed, he followed. It was no concern of hers.

The door closed softly. Julia froze, her hands clenched at her sides. Despite her best intentions, her whole awareness was in questioning whether or not her father had followed her inside. She needed to know.

And then, suddenly, she did know.

He was there, in the room, just behind her. She couldn't see him, but she could feel him standing there, silently watching her.

"I'll get a vase," she said, her voice hoarse. She moved decisively to the counter, a blatant effort to avoid having to look at her father.

"That would be good," her dad said quietly. "You look stressed," he added, then cleared his throat.

Stressed? After the day she'd had so far, *stressed* didn't even begin to describe what she felt. "You could say that."

"Sorry," he apologized abruptly, and then blew out a breath.

She returned with the vase and took the flowers from him. He was still standing. "Forget about it," she replied glibly. "You're only part of the problem. Feel free to sit down if you want."

Her dad took a quick seat in the nearest chair, the stiff blue upright Victorian armchair. He set the present on the corner of the end table, and then shifted several times, looking every bit as uncomfortable as Julia felt.

With a silent prayer for guidance and strength, she pulled herself together and sat down on the couch, opposite her father, and looked him in the eye. The proverbial gauntlet had been thrown, and she deftly picked it up.

"I'm listening," she said sharply. "Talk."

Her father's smile slipped for a moment, but he caught it and twisted his mouth into a sporty half-grin. "You're so much like your mother, Julia. It astounds me. Your beauty, of course. The way you handle yourself. Your composure and self-confidence. All that comes from your mother."

Julia cocked a brow. "I think you should take some of the credit," she said wryly. "For my poor qualities, at least."

He barked out a laugh. "Okay, a little."

Julia found herself relaxing just a little in his presence. It wasn't as hard as she'd imagined it would be, sitting in a room and talking with her father as if he were—well, her *father.*

But she was still a far cry from forgiving and forgetting. That, she thought she might never be able to do.

"I still don't understand why you're here," she said softly, absently pinching the skin between her thumb and forefinger. The discomfort was a welcome distraction.

"I'm here to make amends, Julia. I'm a changed man, and I want to be your father."

"I told you before—I don't want, or need, a father. I'm a grown woman now, and am managing quite nicely on my own."

"I recognize that," Greg agreed immediately. "I don't want to get in your way. I just want to see if it's possible to be a part of your life."

Julia blew out a breath and shook her head. "What? Until you leave again? Until the sweet siren of another job in another town lures you away?"

He nodded sagely. "That might happen."

Julia made a sound half between a laugh and a snort. "That *will* happen. This much I know." She turned her gaze on him, all the anger and frustration of years of abandonment showing in her eyes. "You still can't hold a job for more than a month now, can you?"

He jammed his fingers into the soft curls of his hair and frowned, the first time in very long time Julia had seen such an expression on her father's face.

"Some things don't change."

"Hmmph." Julia shook her head and looked away.

"But my heart is changed, Julia. I found the religion—the relationship—you and your mother treasured so much."

Julia's heart gave an irregular beat, and her breath lodged in her throat. "You're a Christian?"

He nodded rapidly. "Can you believe your old man found the Lord?"

It was a difficult concept to consider. The man who'd trailed in and out of her mother's life, breaking her heart every time he walked out the door, was professing belief in the religion he'd once mocked? The man who'd laughingly made light of his daughter's needs?

Julia shook her head. "I need time. I can't deal with this. I need to think about what you've said, to sort this all out."

Her father stood and nodded, that cocky grin once again perched comfortably on his face. "No problem. You want space, you've got it. But Julia?"

"Hmmm?" she said absently, refusing to meet his eyes.

"Take me seriously."

She balked inwardly. He'd never taken her seriously, so why should she offer him any mercy?

The answer immediately came to her, wrenching her heart in two. *Because that's what Christ would do.*

Chapter Fourteen

The quiet *tick-ticking* of the clock on the mantel bored into Julia's head. She stared again at the present her dad had quietly left on the end table. She hadn't opened it, and wasn't sure if she ever would.

She squeezed the bridge of her nose, dispelling the pressure she felt there. If she didn't get out of here, that clock would drive her insane. Or at least give her one doozy of a headache.

It was too quiet. What else could explain why the generally unobtrusive ticking of the clock was so apparent, and so annoying?

Lakeisha had been gone for nearly a week. She'd bounded off for her trip to her mother's without a single glance backward. Julia wasn't certain her friend had even been aware of her, as caught up as she'd been in the preparations.

Not Christmas preparations. *Leaving* preparations. Not that she blamed her. Who wouldn't want to go home for Christmas?

But now it was Christmas Eve, and Julia was completely and utterly alone.

She was looking forward to the evening, when she would attend Grace Church's traditional Christmas Eve candlelight service. It never failed to warm her heart to hear the revered Christmas story as the Bible told it, gently interspersed with favorite hymns and lovely, majestic pieces performed by the sanctuary choir.

This year, the children were creating a live creche, complete with a donkey and a sheep. Even the baby Jesus would be a living, kicking, perhaps even squalling infant in his mother Mary's arms.

Her mind shifted to Chantelle, who would be coming home to her own mother's arms in just a couple of weeks. God *was* good.

She smiled to herself despite her melancholy. She wasn't the first person to find herself alone on a holiday, and she certainly wouldn't be the last, she told herself firmly.

And she wasn't truly alone, was she?

Didn't God say He'd never leave her or forsake her? Now was as good a time as any to cash in on that holy promise.

Warmth rushed through her. How could she have forgotten God at such a time as this?

Feeling better, and determined to *do* better, she decided she needed to stay busy, and not simply mope about the house. It was several hours before the service, yet.

She would go stir crazy if she remained bottled up in her apartment. Cozy was one thing, but she felt as if she were being suffocated by her surroundings. She curled up on one end of the rumpled sofa, staring out the balcony window toward the snow-glistening Rockies and wondering what she ought to do.

Ice-skating. The abrupt bolt of inspiration surprised her, but she embraced the idea anyway. It had been a good, long while since she'd skated, but what was to stop her from making up for that deficiency this very day!

After all these years, she knew she wouldn't be comfortable enough to skate in front of others, so the local indoor rink was out, but there was that nice pond she'd found tucked in the trees just behind Grace Church, and with the temperature having taken a nosedive in the past few days, she was sure it would be perfect.

She loved to skate. She'd always loved to skate.

Against her will, her mind transported her back to a time deep in her past. How she had begged her father for ice-skating lessons, like all the other little girls in her class were taking. She had such glorious, romantic dreams of becoming a world-famous figure skater, like the ones she'd seen in the Olympic Games on television.

That is, until her father shattered that one tiny ray of hope in an otherwise common existence. Even now, she could hear her mother's words echoing through the recesses of her mind.

There's not enough money this year. Maybe next year, when your father comes home.

But next year hadn't been different, nor the year after that. She'd finally settled with teaching herself the basics with secondhand skates someone in the church had passed down to her when she was fourteen.

Julia stood and stretched, shaking the bittersweet memories from her mind with a wave of her head. Her melancholy mood wasn't going to improve by drudging up old memories.

What would help was going ice-skating. She might not be that world-class figure skater, but she knew enough to have a good time. What better way to spend a lonely winter afternoon?

It had been a while since she'd been on skates, but the movements came back to her with remarkable ease. The crisp bite of the wind in her face, the way her arms floated and bobbed as she turned—it was reminiscent of an earlier, more innocent time.

Julia did a pirouette, laughing when she wobbled and almost fell.

She closed her eyes, reveling in her peaceful surroundings. For a moment, she could almost believe that she was, indeed, a world-class skater. She let her imagination go full force to envision her routine, before finishing with a tuck and bow. In her dream, she could her the crowd roar their applause. She curtsied right, and then left, the warm spotlight glaring upon her. This standing ovation was more than she could ever have dreamed of.

And then she froze, forcefully yanked out of her fantasy by a sound.

There *was* an ovation, albeit singular applause. She spun about, searching for the origin of the all too real appreciation of her efforts.

Zeke Taylor lounged a thick shoulder against the trunk of a solid pine, clapping his approval.

"Bravo," he called enthusiastically. "Encore!"

He appeared genuine enough, but not nearly enough to stop Julia's face from flaming, first from embarrassment at being caught, and then with utter infuriation.

How dare the man interrupt her private moment, and then have the gall to stand there and ridicule her?

Julia very ungracefully stomped off the ice and straight toward Zeke.

"You—you—" she stammered, too flustered to complete her sentence.

Only marginally resisting the urge to thump her

finger into his thick chest, she balled her fists on her hips. ''What on earth are you doing here?''

Zeke's grin widened. He enjoyed her display of temper, knowing she'd merely been caught off guard. He hadn't meant to intrude, but he wasn't the rascal she made him out to be, either.

Not entirely, anyway, he thought, grinning. ''You know you're adorable when you're angry, sweetheart?'' he teased lightly.

Julia's jaw dropped open in astonishment, and he was certain he'd struck a chord within her.

''You know,'' he continued, his throat dry. ''You were pretty good out there. Did you have lessons?'' He grunted as he slid his back down the jagged tree trunk until he was seated on the wet, snow-packed ground.

Julia shook her head, but didn't speak.

''I enjoyed watching you.'' The words were quiet and honest.

She stared at him for a moment before answering. He gazed back at her, waiting patiently for her to answer.

''I wanted lessons,'' Julia said in hushed tones, dropping down beside Zeke and arranging herself primly on the snowbank. ''Daddy didn't make enough money for me to have lessons. Of any nature.''

Zeke nodded. ''That's tough. My folks didn't have much extra money lying around, either.''

Julia scowled suddenly, and shrugged. "Yeah, well, that's in the past now."

With a low sigh, she turned to the burnished sapphire of the glistening pond, her gaze distant and unreadable. Zeke studied her profile, at once struck by her beauty, and aching for the pain she suffered but wouldn't share.

What could he do? Zeke wondered. What could he say? Again, he came up against his own ineptness for words. In the end, he remained silent.

After a moment, she turned back to him. "What are you doing here?"

Zeke took her change in topic in stride, realizing she needed to get away from whatever menace was following her. He hoisted one foot into the air and pointed to his worn black ice skates.

"You're a retired figure skater?" she asked in a teasing tone, the sparkle returning to her glorious green eyes.

Zeke gave a loud chuckle. "I used to play hockey when I was a kid. I haven't been ice-skating in a while, though. It seemed like a good idea today, for some reason."

"Oh." Julia couldn't think of anything to say, so she just shrugged.

"I didn't mean to disturb you," he apologized in a low, rough voice. "It was just an idea. I can come back another time."

"No!" The word was out of her mouth before

Julia could consider the wisdom behind it, but belatedly, she realized her rapid response had been right on the money. ''Please don't leave.''

She *did* want Zeke to stay out here with her. She didn't tolerate Zeke's company—she enjoyed it. She laughed a lot when he was around.

More to the point, up until the moment Zeke arrived, she'd been feeling completely cast aside. That feeling went away when he smiled at her. And it helped a little to know that here was an equally solitary, if not lonesome, human being in the world.

She stood and smiled at him. ''There's more than enough room on this pond for the two of us.''

Zeke returned her smile with his own wide, bearded grin and leaped to his feet, an action remarkably graceful for a man of his size.

''Race you to the far end,'' he called, already skating out over the pond.

''Hey! No fair,'' Julia shouted, quickly pumping her legs to catch up with him.

With his strength, combined with his head start, Zeke was lounging at the far end of the lake, casually practicing a hockey warm-up, by the time Julia glided up, huffing and puffing in the crisp air.

''That's hardly fair,'' she complained, laughing until her sides hurt. ''If anyone should get a handicap here, it's me.''

''With a name like mine, you think *you* should

get the handicap?'' he asked pleasantly. Zeke, she noticed, did not seem the least short of breath.

''Why? What *is* your full name?'' she asked, suddenly curious. She was surprised to see the color heighten on his face above his beard.

Her heart flipped over, leaving her even more short of breath. But he'd been the one to bring it up. She wouldn't back down now. Besides, she really wanted to know.

He pinched his lips together and fidgeted uncomfortably, breaking their locked gaze to look at his feet. ''I've never divulged that information before. To *anyone.*''

''Why not?''

The deep splotches lining his cheeks reddened. ''It's stupid.''

''It can't be that bad,'' she encouraged softly.

''It's bad. Promise you won't laugh.''

Julia reached for his arm and gave it a soft, reassuring caress. ''I'm shocked that you think so little of me,'' she teased. ''Of course I won't laugh at you. I'd never do anything so awful.''

Zeke cringed. ''Famous last words.''

She took that as a personal challenge. ''You think so? Try me.''

He stared at her a moment, then sighed and shrugged grandly. ''Oh, all right. Ezekiel Habakkuk Malachi Taylor.''

Julia's eyes widened, though she tried desperately

to keep her reaction from showing on her face. Laughter bubbled in her throat, and she swallowed. Hard.

Zeke frowned ominously as he searched her expression for any sign of mirth. His twinkling eyes belayed his offended expression, though; the typical paradox of Zeke Taylor. Ezekiel *Habakkuk Malachi* Taylor, she mentally corrected herself, still trying without success to hide her amusement.

For Julia, seeing his dark look was the final straw. She burst into fits of laughter. ''Oh Zeke, how could they?''

Zeke sniffed and planted his hands on his hips, looking all the more masculine for his overstated feminine gesture. ''My mother is very fond of the prophets.''

''I should say so.'' Julia hiccupped, still attempting to control her outburst. It seemed she was constantly laughing when Zeke was near.

''And you?''

''I beg your pardon?''

''I confided *my* middle name—names.''

''Marie.''

He nodded as if satisfied.

''Don't even think about telling anyone else about my name,'' he warned as he slid back onto the ice, gliding in ever widening circles across the pond.

As Julia sped by him, she called out, ''I like your name.''

It was the truth. Zeke was a strong, masculine name, matching the brawny man bearing it. When he reached out his hands, she took them in her own.

"You'll have to name your kids after the Biblical kings or something," she suggested with an impish grin.

He bellowed out a laugh. "What if I have girls?"

She thought for a moment. "Well, the wicked queens are out, so I guess you'll have to go with the more godly Biblical examples of womanhood. Stick with the tried and true, you know? Like Mary Elizabeth or something."

He cocked his head and grinned at her, at once taking in her measure and appearing as if he didn't quite believe what he saw.

Suddenly, his gaze locked with hers, he began swinging her in a slow circle. His mouth was pinched in a tight line, and his brow dropped low over his forehead. It was an expression of intense concentration.

Intense emotion.

He pulled her close, and they promenaded in lazy circles. She was eminently aware of his arm around her waist, of the way his breath mixed with hers as they skated in perfect time with one another.

He didn't speak, and Julia couldn't think of anything to say. But words weren't necessary. It was enough just to be here.

Together.

Suddenly he whirled around in front of her, spanning her waist with his large, gentle hands as he skated backward, pulling her along with him.

"Julia, I..." His breath swirled in the mist as his sentence dangled into nothingness. He pulled her closer, and she realized only belatedly they weren't skating anymore.

Slowly, they skidded to a stop, but Zeke didn't let go of her waist, nor did his intense blue-eyed gaze leave hers, even for a moment.

She knew he was going to kiss her a moment before he cupped her chin in his hands and leaned down to her level.

"Stop me if you..." His mouth hovered close and warm over hers. His voice was low, hoarse, and full of longing.

That hesitation, the simple kindness that made Zeke Taylor the man he was, brought the desperate emotions in Julia's heart to the surface, and it was she who covered that last half-inch, million-mile distance to his lips.

He groaned when their lips met. His kiss, like his touch, was soft and tender, yet she could feel the sheer masculine strength barely constrained beneath the surface.

Zeke might not be a man of words, but he was a man of deep passion, in his faith, in his life and in his love.

Love.

She wondered how long her heart had known what her mind was only now beginning to comprehend.

Her heart pounding loudly in her head, she broke away, skating as fast as she could for the far end of the pond, afraid to look back and see the havoc she'd wreaked by her errant actions.

Her errant heart.

How had this situation gotten so completely out of control? More to the point, how could she ever hope to fix it?

She had to get away. She couldn't face Zeke until she'd had time to calm down. To think. To rationally work through the complications. To straighten out her hopelessly tangled emotions.

She aimed for a small nook where ducks and geese often waded. Perhaps she'd see some today, though the lake was frozen over.

Her mind frantically occupied with trying to get herself out of her awful predicament without hurting Zeke, she didn't even notice the black smudge mottling the otherwise clear surface of the lake until she was right on top of it.

The last thing she remembered hearing before her head started whirling was the terrifying sound of ice cracking under the blade of her left skate, and a deep, alarmed voice screaming her name.

Chapter Fifteen

Time shortened, marked only by the sound of Julia's rapid breathing. Zeke had noted the weak ice earlier, but hadn't thought to mention it to Julia when he was skating with her.

He hadn't been thinking at all, only feeling, from the moment he'd taken Julia into his arms. He mentally kicked himself a million times over for his lack of foresight as he sharply bladed toward Julia.

He knew the danger inherent in black ice, and the knowledge made him pump harder. If he could reach Julia before she fell into the frigid water, they might have a chance.

She hit the ice only moments before he skated to her side. Gritting his teeth and praying desperately, he changed his course and set himself in a straight line for her.

He'd heard the ice crack.

With a final surge of strength, he plowed across the black ice. It broke underneath his blades. With all his might, he catapulted forward, awkwardly grasping Julia in his arms and throwing all his weight in the direction of solid ground.

For a moment, he wasn't certain they'd make it. Then, suddenly, the ground appeared to come up to meet them.

With a grunt, he twisted his body so he took the brunt of the landing, sheltering sweet Julia in his arms as they rolled.

They were safe.

Relief washed over Zeke, and he breathed a prayer of thanks. Reluctantly, he gently released Julia onto the hard ground and rolled onto his back, throwing his arms over his head. The solid, frosty ground felt reassuring under him, and he lay still for a moment and closed his eyes, motionless except for his heaving chest.

He heard Julia beside him as she sat up and rustled around, apparently stretching her own bruised body. She groaned, and his eyes shot open.

"Are you all right?" he asked. He cleared his throat against the scratch in his voice.

"I think so," said Julia, timidly poking at various muscles. "How about you?"

Zeke stood slowly, testing his muscles as he went.

"Nothing broken, but I'm going to be sore when I get up in the morning."

Julia also tried to rise, but fell back with a shriek of alarm. Her face paled markedly, and she squeezed her eyes shut.

"Julia?" Zeke crouched by her side and gently caressed her arm. "Where does it hurt?"

She cringed, giving him no suggestion of from where her pain initiated. "I'm sorry."

"Don't be." His heart swelled. She was so fragile, and she didn't even realize her own limits. Even now her courage showed, as she bit her bottom lip and tried to act as if she weren't in the tremendous pain he knew she was.

Again, she tried to stand, but Zeke pushed her back down. "Where does it hurt?" he asked a second time.

Her gaze met his, tested his, and for a long moment she remained silent.

"My ankle," she said at last, pointing to her left foot. "I must have twisted it when I fell."

He gently probed the area with his fingers, and unlaced her skate as delicately as his big, ungainly hands could manage.

She jerked her leg from his grasp when he touched a tender spot, letting out her first real howl of pain. Then she grew silent, her lips pinched as waves of pain assailed her for her hasty movements.

Zeke again reached for her ankle. "I know this

hurts, sweetheart, but I've got to see what you've done to this ankle of yours.''

He continued to probe deeply, making mental notes when she winced or complained.

For a moment, his exploration ceased as he searched the back pocket of his faded blue jeans for his pocketknife. Taking her foot in a firm grip, he methodically cut the sock away.

''That way I won't have to move your ankle so much,'' he explained as he worked.

Julia's eyes widened, but she kept still, panting deep breaths in order, Zeke surmised, to keep from yanking her leg from his grasp.

''How bad is it?'' she rasped.

''I don't know yet,'' Zeke answered, gently removing the last bits of her sock. With infinite tenderness he replaced her foot on the cool ground, gently packing snow around it to keep it stable.

He'd procrastinated long enough, and Julia was waiting. He crouched down by her and took her hand in his. ''Don't panic, now, sweetheart, but I think it's broken.''

Julia only nodded sullenly.

''I'm going to drive my truck back here so you won't have to be moved so far,'' Zeke said firmly.

''You can do that?'' she asked, gritting her teeth against the pain.

He forced a grin. ''One of the many benefits of a four-wheel drive. My truck can go almost anywhere.'' He paused, and then chucked her lightly under the chin. ''Try not to move any more than you have to.''

Zeke wasn't gone more than a couple of minutes before Julia heard the welcome sound of his engine revving and his boots crackling over the uneven, snow-packed ground.

Moments later he was again by her side, scooping her up as if she weighed nothing, and tucking her into the warmth of his chest. The muscles of his arm contracted and expanded beneath her neck. He smelled fresh and clean, with just a hint of sawdust. A thoroughly masculine scent, she thought dizzily.

Her heart flooded with relief, an emotion she didn't question. She was just so glad Zeke had been here with her. If she'd been alone...

The memory that she'd almost chased Zeke off the pond made her stomach turn over. That she'd been running—skating—away from him at the time of her accident seemed irrelevant now. She gazed up at him, trying to corral her feelings, trying to express her appreciation.

No words came. ''Zeke, I—'' she began, but clamped her mouth shut, unable to continue as, to her chagrin, tears pooled in her eyes.

Zeke's solemn expression turned from compassion to an emotion she couldn't name. His deep-blue eyes sparkled as he, too, fought for words. ''When I saw you skating for that black ice, I...''

Julia nodded. She wasn't surprised or alarmed when Zeke suddenly leaned down to her, claiming her lips in a sweet, sensitive kiss. This time, there was no doubt of the rightness of the action in Julia's heart. Their kiss allowed both of them to express feelings they were unable to voice.

But just as suddenly as he'd kissed her, he withdrew, and Julia wondered if he was remembering their earlier encounter on the pond. Regret filled her for her foolish actions.

He didn't back off physically. His arms were still firmly clutching her to his chest. But his gaze became distant, and his jaw was taut with tension. In a low, gruff voice, he whispered, "I'll try not to hurt you."

He cradled her close in his arms as he lumbered back to the truck. When they reached the big blue work truck, she saw he'd already opened the passenger side door. He deposited her gently onto the seat, taking his time swathing her ankle with a woolen blanket.

His silence was unnerving. Julia tried to read his eyes, but he refused to meet her probing gaze. The tension in the air was thick, punctuated by the tendons straining in his neck.

"Zeke?" she queried gently, just as he was about to close her door.

He froze in his tracks, and then leaned his elbow

against the hood. He looked at her then, his gaze full of regret.

"Julia, I apologize," he said in a coarse but even voice. His throat constricted as he swallowed. Again, he looked away. "I had no right to kiss you. Not out on the ice, and not now. Please forgive me."

He didn't give her time to respond before slamming her door closed and trudging to the driver's side of the truck.

Nor did she have a response to give. If Zeke's kiss was puzzling, his withdrawal was doubly so. She hadn't protested the second kiss. She had, in fact, responded to his touch.

He spoke not a word on the drive to the hospital. Julia puzzled over his reaction and discreetly watched his profile out of the corner of her eye. He was clearly tense. Not that his death grip on the steering wheel was indicative of his overall mood or anything. Or the way he clenched his jaw, for that matter.

In her pain, Julia saw little reason not to direct her pique at the confusing, perplexing man sitting next to her. Maybe it was his fault she could barely think to put two sentences together when she was around him anymore. Maybe it was his fault her knickers were in a twist, and she couldn't figure out right from left, never mind her feelings.

She knew every name she called him was wrong, every accusation false. Did she have to ask forgiveness of someone if she only insulted him in her head?

From time to time he would glance in her direction, and she would look away. She couldn't bear to read the hurt look in his eyes, and know that she was responsible for putting it there. She wanted to scream out an apology, tell him it was all a big mistake, but she was relatively certain he wouldn't respond to such tactics.

Zeke's expression was grim and determined as he scooped her into his arms and carried her gently into the emergency room. The hunted look in his eyes had disappeared, replaced by concern.

He was quick and methodic in his efforts, depositing her in a wheelchair before signing in at the triage center. He didn't leave her side for a moment.

Julia didn't say anything, but she took great comfort in his presence. His large, bulky frame felt like a shelter to her, and his immense heart a wellspring. She prayed he wouldn't leave, but didn't know how to voice her thoughts. Or maybe she was simply afraid.

When the nurse began wheeling her in for examination, Zeke began to follow, then lagged behind, looking from her to the floor and back again. Finally, he halted completely, stuffing his hands in the front pockets of his jeans and watching with wide eyes as the nurse began to wheel her through the emergency room door to the back of the hospital.

"Zeke," she cried, lifting a hand to him, suddenly not caring how it looked to anyone. She was terrified of being alone right now, and Zeke was her only friend.

Relief pouring from his heart, Zeke rushed to her side and took her hand tightly in his, giving it a gentle squeeze to let her know in a tangible way that he was there for her.

He'd started to follow her earlier, only to realize he really had no right. And since Julia hadn't said anything, he'd stopped in his tracks.

"Don't leave me," she begged quietly as he and the nurse helped her up onto the examining table.

"I won't, sweetheart. Just don't move that leg," he reminded her.

His heart was swelling, but his expression was grim. He didn't want his sweet Julia experiencing even a moment of pain, and he suspected she was in for a night of it.

He meant what he said. He wouldn't leave her side.

The nurse bustled around, taking Julia's pulse and blood pressure. "Julia, the doctor will be here in a moment to examine you. And we've already put in a request for you at X ray. Some nights, waiting for an X ray takes forever."

She smiled kindly, and then turned to Zeke. "Are you her husband?"

Zeke felt blood rush to his face, which only intensified at Julia's stunned expression. He cleared his throat. "Uh, no, ma'am. I'm not her husband." He nearly choked on the word. "I'm just a friend."

"Not *just* a friend," Julia corrected quietly.

Zeke's gaze rushed to hers. What did she mean by that? Was she just teasing? Or could she mean that her feelings ran deeper than friendship?

He yanked his red bandanna from his back pocket and mopped the back of his neck. Man, it was hot in here.

The nurse chuckled. "Well, I'll let you two work that one out between yourselves. The doctor will be in shortly."

Zeke turned to Julia, ready to ask her just what she meant by that earlier statement. She'd been light and teasing with the nurse around, but now he saw just how pale her face was, and the distinct shine of pain in her eyes.

There would be plenty of time later to find out if her feelings matched his. For now, he would do as he'd promised, and be there for her—heart, soul, mind and body.

Julia was in the corner of the emergency room, curtained off from the hustle and bustle of the doctors and nurses around her. She'd requested to see Zeke the moment she was out of surgery, and he was reassuringly quick to return to her side.

"How's it feel?" he queried gently, a relieved smile lining his bearded face.

Julia thought he might be hiding a pair of dimples behind that beard of his. That notion made her smile in return, despite all she'd recently been through. "I don't feel anything at the moment. But I have to stay cooped up here until the anesthesia wears off."

Zeke cringed. "It'll probably hurt like a doozy then, huh?" he asked, enveloping her hand in his large one.

"No doubt," Julia agreed. "They put pins and staples and who knows what else in my ankle. I think they said they taped my torn ligaments. Do you suppose they use duct tape?"

Zeke chuckled. "Probably."

Their conversation wore down to an awkward silence for a few minutes.

"I guess we're missing the Christmas Eve service tonight, aren't we?" he asked in a transparent attempt to keep the conversation neutral.

"Oh, Zeke, I'm sorry. You don't need to stay here with me. If you leave right now, you'll still have time to catch at least part of the service."

"No." Zeke surprised her by the vehemence of that single word.

She crooked an eyebrow, waiting for his explanation. *If* he'd give one. He was notorious for his silence.

He grinned crookedly and said more gently, "I

want to stay here with you. Besides, you need a ride home. You didn't bring your car. Remember? And I'm not sure you could drive it now if you had. Do you have a stick shift or an automatic?''

''Automatic,'' Julia replied promptly. ''I never learned how to drive a stick shift. Which is apparently a good thing for me, huh?''

He chuckled. ''I guess.''

''Well, I'm glad you're with me anyway, Zeke.'' She gestured around her. ''Emergency rooms make me nervous.''

''Me, too,'' Zeke said with a relieved laugh. ''I broke my arm once playing football. While I was getting it fixed up, they wheeled in a man who'd had a heart attack. It was just like in the movies—everyone was scrambling around and slamming his chest with those electric pads.''

''How scary for you.'' Julia squeezed his hand. ''How old were you?''

''Twelve. But at least my mom and dad were with me then.''

Julia frowned. If she'd been hurt, she doubted if her father would have bothered to be with her, though of course her mother would have been.

No, that wasn't quite honest. It *had* been her father who'd been by her side during her infrequent childhood illnesses. She remembered him dressing in a silly hat and calling himself *Nurse Daddy.* He did goofy things like that. It was responsibility that was his weak suit. Her heart clenched in pain.

Zeke squeezed her hand, his face a mask of concern. ‘‘Are you hurting?’’

Julia shrugged. ‘‘Yes. But not my foot. My memories. Let’s talk about you.’’

Zeke cocked his head and stared at her as if looking for something. Finally, he capitulated. ‘‘Okay. What about me?’’

‘‘Your mom and dad. Are they...’’ She let her sentence trail, unsure of how to complete it delicately.

‘‘Oh, no,’’ Zeke exclaimed with a nervous chuckle. ‘‘No. I’m grateful to God that both of them are alive and kicking. So much so that they’re out on a Christmas cruise to Alaska at this very moment.’’

‘‘They went on a cruise instead of spending Christmas with their son?’’ Julia demanded, surprised at the surge of righteous indignation flowing through her for the emotional state of her friend.

Zeke chuckled again. ‘‘Sons, plural. I have two younger brothers, but they’re spending the holiday with my Aunt Burma in Palm Springs. Aunt Burma’s a little too much for me.’’

‘‘So you’re all alone this Christmas?’’

Zeke nodded affably. ‘‘Yes. But that’s my own doing. I’m the one who bought the tickets for the cruise. It's something my parents have wanted to do for years. Now just seemed like the right time."

"You can afford a *cruise* on a carpenter's salary?" Julia burst out, and then clapped her hand over her mouth, mortified that her uncharitable thoughts had reached her lips.

"Don't sound so shocked," he protested with a smile, not seeming to take offense. "I didn't make the money in a week, you know."

"I apologize," Julia choked out through a closed throat. "I can't believe I said that. It was none of my business to begin with." Heat poured into her cheeks, and she laughed shakily.

Zeke reached over and tipped her chin up with his finger. His eyes were clear and smiling. "I don't mind your asking," he said firmly. "I'm not touchy about my job. Truth be told, I do make a good living, though I did save for a few months to come up with the cruise money."

He paused and gave her a friendly wink. "Besides, I don't have a family to support. It's just me, and I don't eat all that much."

Julia chuckled, but Zeke's eyes had clouded over, so she quieted. She was unused to seeing his mood change, especially so quickly. He was so often the friendly and open carpenter. Now she was seeing how multifaceted he was, and she was intrigued.

"Why…how did you come to be a carpenter? Is that what your father does?"

Julia watched as his attention shifted from his thoughts to her question. "What? No, my dad's an electrical engineer." Zeke paused and swiped a hand across his face and down his jaw.

When his gaze returned to Julia, the gleam in his eyes that was at once so heart jolting and yet so reassuringly familiar had returned. "This may surprise you, but I have a liberal arts degree."

"You do?" Julia's mouth gaped in spite of herself. Then, realizing how she must look, she immediately apologized. *Again.*

"I'm sorry. I just thought you didn't need a degree to be..." The end of her statement faded into a self-conscious silence.

Zeke chuckled. "You don't have to be afraid to say it. *Carpenter.* Jesus was a carpenter, you know. It's not such a bad vocation, all things considered."

"Why did you go to college, then? I mean, if you didn't need to? Or did you decide to become a carpenter after you finished your degree?"

Zeke thrust his large, callused hands out for her inspection, palms up. They were the strong, worn hands of a man who worked hard for a living.

"I've always been good at making things with my hands. I was the kid on the block who spent most of his time in his dad's workshop. I was always good at math, too, which is important for a carpenter." He stopped and winked at her. "It's an exact science, you know."

A blush warmed her cheeks.

His grin widened. "By the time I was a teenager, I was refinishing antique wood furniture. And making some good money at it, too, which I later used to put myself through college."

Julia marveled that such large hands could be so gentle and nimble with wood. And with animals, like Tip the Wonder Dog.

And especially with people, she reminded herself. She'd have drowned today if it weren't for Zeke.

Hesitantly, she reached out a finger to trace the calluses on one of his palms. He quivered, but didn't remove his hand from her grasp.

"I went to college for my own benefit," he said with a catch in his voice. "I always knew that when I finished I would return to my first love, carpentry."

"You are very fortunate, then," Julia said, feeling the peculiar urge to kiss each worn callus and make it better. "Not many of us have the faintest idea what we want to do with our lives, even in college."

She shook her head. "I wanted to be in an occupation where I could help people, but my forte is art, wouldn't you know. I'm glad you have the opportunity to do what you want to do."

The most surprising thing about her statement was that she really was glad for him.

A *carpenter*.

"I make a good living," he repeated, his eyes warming. Lifting his hands away from her, he shoved them in his pockets and jingled his change as if for emphasis. "I'll be able to take care of a family when the time comes."

When the time comes.

Chapter Sixteen

Zeke couldn't believe she'd let him talk her into going back to the church to retrieve her car. She'd been quite adamant about it, on the verge of hysteria, Zeke thought, and he sure didn't know how to deal with a hysterical woman.

She kept muttering something about having Lakeisha gone, and Julia needing the car in case of an emergency. As if *this* wasn't an emergency.

She had fallen asleep moments after he'd tucked her soundly into his truck, and she'd slept all the way from the hospital to the church parking lot. Her head had slipped comfortably onto his shoulder, and he hesitated to disturb the pretty scene she made.

Sometimes his heart just ached, full as it was with his love for Julia. If only he could find the words to tell her how he felt.

He turned off the engine and flicked off the lights, but didn't wake Julia immediately. The parking lot was much as they had left it, but there were signs of the many people who'd come to worship at Grace Church that evening.

Festive green and red bulletins littered the parking lot here and there. A few used candles were strewn across the side of the stairs.

"I'm sorry you missed it."

Zeke nearly jumped out of his skin at Julia's soft, compassionate whisper.

"Missed what?" he said, noting the coarse, sandpaper quality of his voice.

"Christmas Eve."

"I didn't miss Christmas Eve," he objected. "It's right here in front of us."

"I meant the service, and you know it," she said, playfully poking him in the rib as she sat back up and stretched. "I really wanted to be there tonight."

"I'm sorry you missed it," he said, reaching out to brush back a lock of stray hair that had fallen over Julia's face.

"I wish I could at least go in and pray for a minute."

Zeke brightened. "Merry Christmas."

"Merry Christmas to you, too."

"No. I mean, I can grant you your wish."

Her gaze narrowed on him in the soft darkness of the night. "How?"

He pulled his key from the ignition and jangled the key chain in front of her. ‘‘Your wish is my command.’’ And he was happy to do it, for in bringing Julia happiness, he found it himself.

He helped her out of the truck. She wanted to try walking on her new crutches, but Zeke would have none of it. Not with the number of ice patches shining on the asphalt.

Besides, why should she walk when he could easily carry her in the comfort of his arms?

She squealed as he scooped her up. ‘‘Did I hurt you?’’ he asked, creasing his forehead.

‘‘Hurt me? No,’’ she said with a small laugh. ‘‘But you startled the living daylights out of me.’’

‘‘Sorry.’’ He did his best to look repentant, and knew he'd failed when she laughed.

He brought her into the church and headed for the sanctuary.

‘‘Why do you have keys to the church?’’ she asked suddenly. ‘‘I mean, I'm not surprised, but I didn't know you performed in some official capacity here.’’

‘‘I don't,’’ he said evenly. ‘‘It's nothing official. I just do the odds and ends repairs over here, so they gave me a key.’’

Julia nodded. She'd suspected it was something like that—official capacity wasn't Zeke's style. Yet he did twice as much for others as most official ministers she knew.

"Where do you want me to put you?" Zeke asked, flipping on the lights to the sanctuary.

"Well, I can't kneel," Julia said. "In fact, the kneelers are going to be hard to manage, even without kneeling."

"I guess that leaves kneeling at the altar out, too, huh?" Zeke asked, looking around for a solution.

"Just deposit me in the front row," Julia instructed.

"Can I take you back with interest?"

"What? Oh..." Julia's face flamed at his gentle teasing.

For all his banter, Zeke was quick to leave her alone in the sanctuary. Alone with her thoughts, and her feelings, all of which banked up against each other like puppies raring to get out of their pen.

She stared up at the cross on the wall, then down at the remnants of the nativity scene across the base of the altar platform.

As always, the contrast of the scene struck her heart. A king who was born a pauper. God made Man to die for man, a thief's death on a Roman cross. And yet tonight was for celebrating, gifts given to loved ones in remembrance of Jesus' great gift to mankind.

Grateful tears coursed down her cheeks as she realized she wasn't alone, and hadn't ever been alone, even when she was at her loneliest. Surely a baby born in a manger must have known many tears.

He knew.

She closed her eyes. She wanted to release all her fear and sorrow, but even now she was afraid. How could she possibly deserve what God freely gave?

"Are you hurt?" Zeke asked from somewhere in the darkness, his voice lined with concern. "Is it your leg?"

Julia laughed dryly and swiped at her tears as Zeke came forward into the light. "No, not my leg. My heart." She hiccupped a breath. "But I'll be fine, now. I'm not alone."

"No, you're not," Zeke agreed gruffly as he swept her back into the warmth of his arms. "Never alone, Julia. Do you understand?"

"I think I'm beginning to." She paused for a moment. "How did you know I was crying?"

He squeezed her tight to his chest. "The acoustics in the sanctuary are pretty good."

"I guess."

He paused and set her down on the front steps as he turned back to check the lights and lock up the place.

For after midnight, it wasn't cold. The building and surrounding trees blocked any gusting wind. Julia swept in a deep, clean breath of air, and then let it out with a sigh.

"Still sad?" Zeke asked, slipping down next to her on the stairs.

"Not sad," she denied softly. "Though I still

wish I could have been here when they lit the candles.''

Without a word, Zeke stood and hopped over the side rail. Julia's jaw dropped in astonishment—the drop was four feet if it was an inch. She heard him rustling around and assumed that meant he wasn't hurt.

Hurt? The man was made of steel. She crooked a smile at the thought of the worry that had coursed through her when he'd disappeared over the railing.

''Are you sneaking off without me to leave me to freeze in the snow?'' she called into the blackness of the night. She wished there was a moon, so she could see better.

Suddenly he was beside her, one hand behind his back and looking very pleased with himself, and her. ''No, not leaving.''

''What, then?'' she asked, smiling at his secretiveness, her heart beginning to pound with a childlike sense of anticipation.

He pulled his hand forward. It contained two candles, apparently discarded after the candlelight service earlier.

Her breath caught and held as he gently opened her palm and placed once of the candles in her hand. With a soft touch undergirded by his strength, he wrapped her fingers around the stem, then turned her hand until he could brush a soft kiss against back of her knuckles.

She couldn't see his expression in the darkness, but she could clearly see the tender, reverent look in his eyes, as he fished in his pocket for a box of matches, and then scratched one, sending a single bright flame flickering around his face.

The breath locked in her throat let out in a whoosh as her heart expanded to fill every gap in her chest. Quietly, reverently, Zeke lit his own candle, and then blew the match out.

He put his free arm around her and brought his head close to hers, so close his warm breath fanned her cheek.

He looked as if he were preparing to say something, but at the last moment, he simply tipped his candle into hers, so that their flame became one as her fire was lit with his.

She watched the flames for a moment, thanking God for this time, for Zeke, for Jesus, the Baby and the King.

It was Zeke who broke the silence. She'd never heard his voice sound more regal or majestic as when he offered the simple song of gratitude up to God.

Reverently, lovingly, she joined in.

"Silent night, Holy night..."

Julia awoke to the crackling sound and pungent aroma of bacon frying on the range. At first her foggy brain registered little other than the tantalizing suggestion of breakfast.

For a moment, she almost believed she was still a child, and the homey sounds coming from the kitchen were those of her mother joyfully cooking the family's traditional Christmas breakfast: blueberry muffins, scrambled eggs and bacon, all washed down with fresh orange juice.

Her father would call her down to breakfast, and she'd race down the stairs, anxious to begin tearing into the gifts than surrounded the fresh-cut Christmas pine. Most of the gifts would be hers.

"Mmm," she said, yawning and stretching. Instantly, she froze her movements, not so much because of her aching muscles, of which there were many, but because of the sharp pain that pierced up her left leg.

Reality thrust its ugly nose into her pleasant childhood memories, reminding her forcefully that she was now an adult. And she was alone on this Christmas morning—or at least, she was supposed to be.

Who on earth was in her kitchen? She was curious, but not frightened. Burglars didn't fix breakfast.

Perhaps Lakeisha had returned early. She set her jaw against the continued throbbing in her ankle and turned onto her back, resting her head in the crook of her arm.

"Good morning, sleepyhead," called Zeke from outside her closed bedroom door. "I borrowed your key and let myself in this morning. I thought you might like to have a nice breakfast for Christmas morning. Can you get yourself up to the table?''

Julia jolted when she heard a male voice on the other side of the door, sending her heart racing, and bringing a smile to her lips—at least until she tried to move.

The first attempt brought a shock of pain, and she groaned. With effort, she managed to slide to the edge of her bed and wrestle her protesting body into a sitting position. She was still wearing the faded jeans and red shaker sweater of the night before. At the time, it had seemed easier to sleep in her clothes than to change.

She'd been exhausted when Zeke had dropped her off the night before, and, after taking a pill for the pain, had fallen into a dead sleep the moment her head hit the pillow, despite the cast on her leg. Zeke, she assumed, had let himself out.

''It smells wonderful,'' Julia called back, taking a deep whiff of what she was sure was fresh-baked blueberry muffins. ''I'll be along as quickly as I can.''

''No rush,'' he called. ''Whenever you're ready.''

She could hear him whistling ''Joy to the World'' as he worked, pots and pans clamoring, followed by the familiar high-pitched *ting* of plates and silverware meeting.

Julia reached for her crutches and made the painful journey to the bathroom, muttering under her breath at her pallid skin that amplified the black shadows resting under her eyes. She scrubbed her face vigorously with a warm, damp cloth, hoping to restore some color, then debated whether or not to apply makeup.

Her growling stomach won out over the desire to look pretty for Zeke. The tantalizing smells reminded her all too well that she'd missed supper the night before.

Besides, Zeke had already seen her both without makeup and at her worst. If he couldn't handle it, he probably would have already left, she thought with a smile.

The first thing she noticed upon entering the alcove that contained the dining room table was the huge vase of bright-pink carnations—at least two dozen of them—that nearly overwhelmed the modest round table.

Zeke stood at the kitchen sink, his back turned to her, Tip resting quietly at his feet. She didn't resist the urge to lean her face into the bouquet and take a deep whiff of the intoxicating scent. As she straightened, she noticed a small card attached to one of the stems.

She swept a furtive glance at Zeke, but he was still busy at the sink. Balancing on one crutch, she opened the tiny envelope. The card read, "May your future be running over with God's blessing."

She swept in a breath and held it as she read the simple signature—*Love, Zeke.*

Julia stared at the card for a full minute before placing it gently on the table before her. Here were the pink carnations she'd been waiting her whole life to receive, a token of sentiments she had once fervently vowed she wanted nothing to do with.

And yet, she thought, her heart giving a regretful twinge, this wasn't how it was supposed to be at all. Zeke Taylor was too good a man for her Great Scheme.

Somehow, Zeke had known her preference for pink carnations. Or maybe it was a fluke. But either way, the flowers signified some indication of his feelings for her. Didn't they?

Julia's mind was in a muddle. Zeke was a dear friend, perhaps the best one she'd ever had. He listened. He cared.

And so, she realized, did she.

"Zeke, these carnations are lovely," she said, wincing at the betraying squeak in her voice.

Zeke turned from the sink, holding his wet arms at shoulder level.

Julia immediately burst out laughing.

"What's so funny?" he asked, cocking a hip and pretending offense. He was dressed in his usual blue jeans and a black flannel shirt. But what caught her eye the most was her own white, frilly, lacy apron draped around Zeke's shoulders, barely serving to protect the center of his chest, dwarfed against his upper body.

"Now don't you go thinking I'm getting soft and frilly on you," he drawled, throwing his wet hands to his hips.

"Of course not," Julia agreed. "I'd never think of suggesting such a thing."

And she wouldn't, either. The frilly apron was funny precisely because it looked so ridiculous on Zeke's masculine frame. Zeke was, she admitted frankly to herself, without a doubt the most attractive, masculine man she had ever met.

And she *was* attracted to him. Not only were his features handsome, but his quiet, gentle strength and faith, and the integrity with which he lived, gave him a distinct appeal that the other men she knew lacked.

She fervently wished Lakeisha hadn't run off to her mother's for Christmas. Julia definitely needed a friend to talk with right now. Her life was becoming more complicated by the moment.

If, emphasis on *if,* she was falling in love with Zeke, she was headed for sheer disaster, and she didn't know how to apply the brakes. Not that Lakeisha was an expert on love, but at least she was a true believer in love, and insisted on the benefits of having love catch you off guard.

The most frightening thing of all was that falling

in love was beginning to sound like a winning deal. When she thought about Zeke, it became appealing to follow the whims of her heart, and her Great Scheme be burned.

Chapter Seventeen

"Dig in," Zeke encouraged with a crooked grin. She looked nearly as dazed as she had when she'd first appeared in the kitchen.

He knew he was taking a big chance in coming here this morning, but it was a risk he had to take. He well knew he was stepping over the boundaries she'd laid. She'd have every right to be angry with him if she wanted to be. He'd even brought his dog without asking.

But there was no one here to care for Julia, and it was Christmas morning. No one should be alone on Christmas morning.

Not even him.

With the first bite, Julia began eating ravenously, if in her usual elegant manner. "This breakfast is just what the doctor ordered,'' she said in between bites.

They ate heartily, both having missed supper the night before. Even Tip dug into her small plate of bacon on the floor. Julia kept up a steady stream of small talk between mouthfuls, hardly letting him get a word in edgewise. That suited Zeke just fine. He liked to listen to the melodic sound of her voice. And he didn't know what to say, anyway.

His heart welled in his chest, until he thought he might burst with the feelings Julia fashioned inside him. He prayed desperately for control. As much as he loved Julia, he wanted first to glorify God.

But hadn't God put these feelings for Julia in his heart? Peace and joy washed over him as he realized it was true. There was no barrier between him and his love for Julia.

Except, perhaps, Julia herself. He knew she felt something for him, but was that something strong enough to stand the test of time? Last night, they'd shared the most intimate moment of his life. He could only hope she felt the same way.

But it wasn't enough to wonder. Suddenly, and with all his heart, he had to know.

He pushed back his chair and stood slowly, then stacked the empty plates. ''Julia, I need to talk to you,'' he began, feeling as out of breath as if he'd run a marathon. ''I have something to tell you.''

He struggled to keep his features composed as he

brought the dirty dishes to the sink. He wanted to grin like a schoolboy. But he paced himself and turned, setting his jaw with determination.

She needed to know how he felt. Now.

"I know it's Christmas morning and all, and neither one of us got a good night's sleep. Still, we're alone here this morning, and I feel I've got to speak while I'm still able to do so."

He lumbered to her side. With another grin, he lifted her softly and placed her on the couch, and then crouched before her. He wasn't even aware he'd been holding his breath until his lungs began to burn from lack of oxygen. He gulped for air.

"What's up?" Her usually sunny soprano was stilted, a sure sign that her throat was constricting around her words.

He swallowed hard. He was a man of action, not words, and especially not talking about relationships and feelings. He was way out of his element.

He wanted to tell her how he'd been attracted to her by her honesty and lack of guile. How he'd watched her serve others without a thought to herself. Her kind heart and commitment to God would make any man's heart melt. She was a woman a man would be proud to stand by, to love and protect and serve.

His heart hammered so strongly in his chest he was certain Julia must be able to hear it. Would that she'd be able to hear his thoughts, also, so that he would not have to go through the painful process of making them words.

She sat patiently, varying emotions fighting for prominence in her expression. A sense of unreality enveloped him, making his head swirl. None of this was planned.

"Zeke, don't," Julia protested suddenly, her voice cracking. "Please don't."

Zeke put up his hands, palms out, as if to ward off a blow. "No. Don't stop me. It's something that needs to be said, to clear the air between us. After that, I promise I won't say another word about it."

Julia, for once, was struck completely dumb.

"I'm in love with you, Julia. I think I always have been. I love everything about you. Like how your cute little nose perks on the end."

Despite herself, she raised a hand to shield her nose from his view.

Zeke chuckled.

So many feelings welled up in Julia she thought she might twist away like a tornado. Every little thing was out of control, and panic surged through her.

"But even more than your outer beauty," he continued, "I love the beauty of your soul, which tells me so much about your true heart for God."

A tear ran unheeded down Julia's cheek, leaving a slight, glistening trail in its wake. Zeke reached across the open space between them and gently wiped the streak away with the corner of this thumb. It was the lightest of caresses, yet it sent shivers down Julia's back in a way cold air could never do.

"It would give me the greatest pleasure on this earth to have you for my wife, to hold you and cherish you the way you deserve to be cherished, every single day for the rest of my life. My work would be an extra joy just to be providing for you. I'd give you everything I have. Everything I am."

"Oh, Zeke," Julia begged, her heart wrenching with every word he spoke. "Please don't. Not now." There were too many questions unanswered, problems unsolved.

She couldn't seriously think about a significant relationship with Zeke, with her relationship with her father—and her heavenly Father—at such cross purposes. She was terrified. He was asking her to marry for love.

She squeezed her eyes shut against the pain throbbing in her temple.

"Why not now?"

"I have...other issues I need to resolve. There's someone else I—"

"I'm not asking you to marry me," Zeke interjected hastily. His gaze took on a glazed distant quality.

Julia tried to speak, but it came out a croak.

He strode to the front closet and reached for his coat. "I just wanted you to know how I feel. I love you. I always will. If you ever need anything, I'll be there for you. You don't even have to ask.''

She knew with a stark certainty the truth of his words. He *would* be there for her, as he had been since they'd begun their friendship.

She watched him walk away, his steps sturdy and firm. She longed to call for him as he swung through the door, to beg him not to leave. To ask the question her heart so wanted to answer.

But something deep inside smothered her words before they could reach her lips. She wouldn't—couldn't—ask, or answer, even though she knew that as Zeke walked away, he took her heart along with him.

Julia had apparently dozed off on the couch, her head resting in her hands. She woke suddenly when the door to the apartment crashed open.

Lakeisha stumbled in the door, looking entirely too cheerful. Her normally neat black hair looked windblown, though the day was calm.

Julia stood abruptly, apparently forgetting in the rush, her broken ankle. But the pain shooting up her leg was clearly a sharp reminder, and she sat back, her face pallid.

''What happened?'' Lakeisha burst out, rushing to her side. ''Are you okay?''

Julia laughed shakily. ''That depends on your definition of *okay*. My ankle is broken.''

"Oh, you poor baby." Lakeisha gave her a big hug, patting her back like a mother would a child.

"I think my heart is broken, too," Julia admitted softly. "And that hurts even worse." She ceased speaking when hot tears sprang to her eyes.

"What happened? Tell me everything," Lakeisha demanded.

"Wait," she inserted hastily. She'd wished for Lakeisha to be here, but now that she was, Julia wasn't sure she could talk about what had happened. "Why are you here?"

Lakeisha snorted. "Well, that's a fine how-de-do. I'm glad you missed me."

Despite herself, Julia chuckled. "That's not what I meant and you know it. Why are you back *early?*" she modified.

Lakeisha waved her hand in a brushing motion. "Mom and Robert got married. Hitched. On Christmas Eve. It was so great!"

"I'm happy for them."

"So am I," Lakeisha agreed. "But then I figured they needed a honeymoon, so I came home. I sure didn't expect to find you all laid up."

Julia shrugged. "It's not so bad. How *did* you get home, by the way?"

"I stood on standby forever and caught the earliest possible flight, which, let me tell you, was no easy feat—not with all the holiday traveling. Good thing I had my credit card."

"I guess," Julia agreed mildly. "There's still some warm blueberry muffins left in a basket in the kitchen, along with some bacon, if you're hungry."

"Great! I'm famished," Lakeisha exclaimed, already on her way to the kitchen. "You cooked with a broken ankle?"

Julia took a sudden interest in examining her cast. "Zeke cooked me breakfast."

"Zeke Taylor cooked you breakfast on Christmas morning?" She let out a low whistle. "Just look what happens when I leave for a couple weeks."

"It's not that big of a deal," Julia said, and then cringed with the lie.

Lakeisha sauntered back into the living room, nibbling on a muffin with a smug, thoughtful expression on her face. "All right, girlfriend. What gives?"

Julia smiled. She related the story of her ice-skating adventure and how Zeke had rescued her, leaving out the fact that he'd kissed her, as well as their time at the church, which felt almost sacred. Those secrets were too private to share, even with her roommate and dear friend.

"You're blushing," Lakeisha said wryly. "Which brings me to the question that has been gnawing at my mind since I barged in here earlier."

"What?"

"Something happened. Something big."

''Sort of,'' Julia admitted, unable to hide her confusion.

''Big *how?*'' Lakeisha asked, her eyes narrowing like a detective closing in on a big case. ''What did he do, propose?''

Julia knew Lakeisha meant it as a joke, which made it that much more of a shock to her system. ''Not exactly,'' she hedged.

''He *proposed* to you!'' Lakeisha exclaimed, dancing about the room with a muffin in each hand. ''You and Zeke! I just knew it. I knew it all along. Didn't I say it would happen? Zeke's the man for you, I said. I called it from the first. Oh, Julia, I'm so happy for you.'' She embraced Julia so firmly that it sent shooting pains up her cast-covered leg.

She groaned. ''I hate to burst your bubble,'' said Julia, thoroughly exasperated and in no small measure of pain. It had been a *long* day. ''But it occurs to me to point out that I have no intention of marrying Zeke Taylor!''

''What?'' If Lakeisha had almost screamed before, her voice definitely raised a few decibels now. ''What do you mean you aren't going to marry him? Are you crazy?''

''Probably,'' Julia agreed shakily, sinking back into the warmth of the sofa. ''I don't think I am meant to get married at all. To be honest, I don't know that what I feel for Zeke is love. But I will admit there is something between us. I care very much for him. But I'm not going to marry him. I'm sorry if this hurts, Lakeisha. But people who marry for love get hurt, and that's a fact. I'm not going to make the same mistake my mother made.''

''Zeke isn't your father, Julia,'' Lakeisha said quietly. She rested her arm across the back of the sofa and tucked her legs underneath her. ''And even if he *was* like your father, which he's not...''

Julia held her hand up, but Lakeisha pressed on.

''I know you don't want to hear this, Julia, but your Mom was in love with your father, with all his quirks and faults. I think if you search deep within your heart, you'll find that you love Zeke Taylor.

''If you're honest with yourself, you'll realize that you two have exactly what it takes to build a lifetime relationship. Something different and better than what your parents shared. And something completely different than your *Great Scheme,* which was nothing more than a way to ease your conscience and satisfy the ticking of your biological clock. You have a chance at true happiness, Julia. All you have to do is let it happen. Zeke would never hurt you the way your father hurt your mom. And I can tell you one thing—if a man of Zeke's caliber ever proposes to me, I'm not going to be wearing that long look covering your face.''

She paused, shaking her head regretfully. ''Not me, honey. I'll be packing my bags for my honeymoon.''

Chapter Eighteen

The next few days saw a steady stream of visitors to wish Julia well. Many people from HeartBeat and Grace Church stopped by, often bringing flowers or balloons or meals to help her out. Even Thomas and Evy Martin dropped in, promising they'd bring Chantelle over when she was released from the hospital in a few days.

Zeke stopped by daily, but never stayed long, and never attempted to corner her alone or bring up the subject he'd been so intent on Christmas morning.

Which was a good thing, for Julia was on her guard against such a circumstance occurring. She was determined not to give Zeke the opportunity to propose.

If he didn't ask, she wouldn't have to endure the blinding pain of turning him down.

She was getting heartily tired of always having to be waited on. She felt like an invalid on crutches.

This wasn't supposed to be a big deal, was it? Didn't people break their legs every day?

But after a week, she still wasn't able to do much other than move back and forth between her bedroom and the living room sofa, and even that was with little grace. She felt like a hog-tied calf, so awkward were her movements.

Sighing loudly, she reached down and picked up the present her father had left when he was here. She'd tried to open it several times, only to change her mind and put it down untouched. She just couldn't bring herself to see what was inside, to find what her father considered a present to a daughter he barely knew. Now, again, she fingered the clumsily wrapped gift. The midnight-blue paper boasted angels trumpeting the birth of Christ, and again Julia remembered her father's halting confession of faith.

Could it be true?

The present felt like a book, except that it was too soft around the edges. Curiosity overcame her. Biting the edge of her lip, she tore into the paper, and then gasped in surprise as tears sprang to her eyes.

Her mother's worn leather Bible, just as she remembered it as a child. Years washed away as she pictured her mother curled in an armchair, the Bible open on her lap.

She stared misty-eyed at the gold-embossed words on the cover.

Holy Bible.

It had been her mother who'd passed down the faith of the fathers to her. She swallowed hard.

Jesus was supposed to be her rock, her fortress in times of trouble. In her mind she had known that for years, yet the words had never touched her heart.

Not until this moment.

If ever there was a time when she needed a rock to cling to, it was now. She was drowning in a sea of her own making.

She flipped idly through the pages, wondering where to turn for help. All the precious words, the chapters, the books, were entirely familiar to her, and yet so completely foreign.

She ruffled the gilt-edged pages. There were so many words. How would she find what she needed?

God help me, she prayed desperately. God was her final hope in sorting out the mess she was in. She prayed silently, ashamed that He had been the last place she'd turned in her trouble.

Perhaps her walk with the Lord wasn't everything she'd convinced herself it was, even, maybe even in spite of, her constant search to do more for Him, to be more for Him.

As she meandered through her mother's Bible, her gaze alighted on a small red rose petal flattened between the pages in the book of Ephesians. With it was the corner of a torn and time-stained piece of stationary.

Without considering whether or not she should, she flattened the Bible so she could read the faded words.

To Greg, my love.

She swallowed hard. It was a love letter, written long ago by her mother, and to her father. She knew she was trespassing into private territory, yet she found herself unable to stop reading. Further memories of the many wonderful years with her mother engulfed her.

It was almost as if her mother had reached down from heaven and caressed Julia's soul as she read her mother's words to her father: "I'll cherish every moment God allows us to share. Know that every moment we're apart, my heart is yet with you."

Julia's tears wet the seasoned page, further blotching the ink. She turned the sheet over hastily, wanting to preserve the precious memento.

Her mother hadn't been blind to what her father was. She'd loved him through it. It turned Julia's understanding of her parents' relationship over on its end. If her mother had known and forgiven Greg Evans of his faults, could she, Julia, do any less?

Her eyes lighted on a couple of verses in the second chapter of Ephesians, words that had been highlighted with a bright yellow pen: "For by grace you have been saved through faith, and that not of yourselves, it is the gift of God, not of works, lest anyone should boast.''

The words were not new to Julia. They were the first verses she had ever memorized—for a contest in her junior high youth group. She closed her eyes, able to see the words clearly imprinted in her mind. She hadn't forgotten those verses in all these years.

Or had she?

Not of works, lest anyone should boast.

The words echoed over and over in her mind.

Not of works.

Not of works.

The verse was talking about salvation. Salvation was the free gift of God in Christ.

But what about afterward? What about now?

Her head throbbed and pounded. Hadn't she been trying to *do* for God? Wasn't she working for Him? Or had she been trying to collect brownie points for heaven?

Her Great Scheme might have been just another notch on her Bible.

She felt the tingling of a thousand tiny shivers running up her back. The answer she'd been searching for was right here before her. She read the words again.

Not of works.

She didn't have to carry the burden she'd been bearing all this time. Christ was waiting to take it from her. It was as if the sun had risen after a moonless night, so clear did her mind and heart suddenly become.

Being a Christian was a relationship with God, not fulfilling a *Things to Do* list.

She closed her eyes again, this time savoring the warmth and peace running through her. How had she possibly forgotten her love for God?

But now it was back. She was back. And she knew most assuredly that she could face whatever problems and trials now assailed her. She was ready to take advantage of all the good happening in her life.

Julia was finally ready to accept what her heart had been telling her for weeks.

She loved Zeke Taylor.

And he loved her.

That she could be so magnificently blessed caused her heart to swell into her throat, and she sent silent prayers of thanksgiving heavenward. She and Zeke would spend their lives together, and have a beautiful family together.

She wondered how many children Zeke wanted. Julia herself had never given that much thought to children, but now the prospect of a family of little blond-haired, blue-eyed children that resembled their father wasn't so very daunting.

No matter what, she knew they'd be happy.

Outrageously, wonderfully happy. As her parents had been in their own way, if she'd only opened up her eyes and looked. Only they would do it better. That was her father's gift to her.

The power of her emotions nearly overwhelmed her. She thought blithely that they'd have to start their family right away; otherwise her heart would surely burst from the love bubbling inside. Her children, *their* children, would be further outlets in which to pour out her happiness and love.

She couldn't wait to tell Zeke.

But first, she had a phone call to make.

Someone thumped loudly on the door, and Julia stirred from where she lay on the couch, her mother's Bible propped open in her lap. It had been two days, and so far her plans had come to nothing.

"You sure are popular," Lakeisha complained, scuffling from the bedroom. She waved her hands back and forth, her fingers spread wide, looking rather like she was attempting to conduct a symphony.

"Just painted your fingernails?" Julia guessed correctly, with a laugh.

"And they are going to smudge when I answer the door, thank you very much," quipped Lakeisha, who nevertheless grappled for the doorknob. "Come in, come in. Welcome visitors, and all that."

Julia's father swept a ball cap off his head and entered the apartment, just as Julia struggled to a sitting position from where she reclined on the faded and quite lumpy sofa. She had never before noticed how the worn inner fibers had bunched over time, leaving the sofa bumpy and abrasive on her tender skin.

It was just enough to put her out of sorts, she thought, were she not so glad to see her father.

Lakeisha looked dazed, as if unsure whether to invite the prodigal father in, or to slam the door on his face.

"Come on in, Dad," Julia called to ease Lakeisha's burden. She thanked God for a friend who cared as much as Lakeisha, who understood and reflected her own feelings. But now her feelings had changed.

Her father's gaze brushed over her before resting on her cast. He looked ready to drop from exhaustion, Julia thought, noticing the dark circles under his eyes, the exaggerated crow's feet around his eyes.

He looked so much older than she remembered the last time she'd seen him.

Yet in spite of his fatigue, he moved with the agility and grace of a much younger man as he rushed to his daughter's side, awkwardly grasping her hands in his.

"Julia, baby, what happened?" The years and empty space between them dissolved, he curled her into his chest just as he had done when she was a child, a time when she had truly believed Daddy could heal all her wounds.

For a brief moment, Julia allowed herself to believe it again.

"It was nothing," Julia said, clumsily removing herself from his embrace. She proceeded to fill him in on her accident.

They sat in awkward silence for several minutes. Julia was more than a little concerned about her father's haggard appearance, but was unsure how to voice her thoughts. It had been too many years, and she'd kept too much distance between them. How would she ever bridge the gap now?

A few weeks ago she would have blurted her thoughts right out, probably in anger. But things had changed for her over this short time.

She had changed, she realized in astonishment.

The front door opened quietly, causing both of them to turn. Julia's father stood haltingly, his eyes widening at the apparent familiarity with which the giant of a man entered the apartment.

Zeke let himself in, then turned, startled to find himself face-to-face with the older man. That Julia had company was no big surprise, but that it was the familiar face of the Grace Church janitor—Julia's father—stunned him to the core.

He glanced at Julia, and she nodded in response to his unspoken question.

"Greg," he boomed out, extending his hand. "How are you?"

"Zeke," Julia's father replied, flashing a friendly smile. "Are you here to see my Julia?"

Zeke saw Julia bristle, and encouraged her with a wink.

"Yes, sir, I'm here to see Julia," he said easily. Speaking to Julia, he said, "I let myself in. I thought you might be dozing."

He also knew how stir-crazy she was, and he thought she might just chuck her pillow at him.

"How are you feeling, sweetheart?"

Julia blushed at the use of his familiar pet name, and his smile widened. He shouldn't tease her like this, but it was just too good an opportunity.

Her father seemed to be taking it in stride, reseating himself on the armchair, which left open the opposite side of the sofa from where Zeke stood. The seat right next to Julia.

Before being seated himself, he asked politely, "Is this a bad time for me to be here, Greg? I know you haven't seen your daughter in a while. I can always come back another time."

"Not at all, Zeke. We'd like you to join us, wouldn't we, Julia?"

Zeke seated himself without waiting for her answer, though he thought she'd be happy to have him there. As far as he knew, she still wasn't on speaking terms with the man.

With Zeke to break the tension, the three spoke easily of her father's recent traveling experiences and Zeke and Julia's ice-skating escapade. Her father roared with laughter at Zeke's description of his own role as the knight in shining armor. And his eyes narrowed with concern as Zeke described spending Christmas Eve in the emergency room of a hospital.

Julia was finally beginning to relax in her father's presence, very much due to Zeke's easy manner with Greg. As usual, Zeke knew all the right things to say to put anyone at ease, including her father.

After several minutes, Julia's father cleared his throat. "I'm sure you'll understand if I request to see Julia alone for a few minutes," he said without preamble. "It's important, Zeke, or I wouldn't ask."

Zeke wasn't too quick to jump when Greg requested it. He gave Julia a long, hard look, apparently trying to access her feelings on the matter. She couldn't mistake the ardent devotion in his gaze, not even if she wanted to, and knew he would stay here with her if she so much as nodded.

Of course, he couldn't know she'd invited her father here herself. "Please, just go," she whispered, a ragged tone to her voice.

For a moment, Zeke's face registered a kind of hurt surprise, but then he locked his featured into a clear line. Even then, his smoky blue eyes held a glimmer of his intent. He wanted to remain her protector, and she was, in a very real sense, sending him away.

She didn't miss the way he slammed the door behind him. Her heart ached as if a door had slammed there, as well.

"So, then, what's the deal with Zeke?" her father questioned, reminding Julia of a similar question from her roommate's lips. It was a question that continued to haunt her late at night when she was unable to sleep.

"What about Zeke?" she echoed testily, not wanting to blurt out something foolish to her father.

"Just wondering if there's anything serious going on between the two of you," he answered, point-blank.

"Yes," she answered before she thought better of it. "No," she amended hastily.

Her father chuckled. "Which is it? Yes or no?"

Julia groaned. "I wish I knew."

"That bad, huh?"

"Worse."

"Love never comes easy, hon," her father said softly, his head bent. "There's always a price."

Julia's gaze riveted to him, but he wouldn't look up and meet her eyes. She'd always pictured him as the aggressor, the one who administered the pain, but now she saw him as he was, a man filled with pain and regret for actions he couldn't take back.

She'd hated this man. Now she felt only pity. And love.

Reaching for her mother's Bible, which was still lying open on the coffee table, Greg Evans reached out and ran a finger across the highlighted verses in Ephesians.

"These were your mother's favorite verses," he said, a catch in his voice. "That's why I put the note and rose petal between those pages. The words always remind me of your mother."

Her father's words heightened her joy. Julia's heart swelled with love for her departed mother, feeling her love reaching out to her even through the distance of eternity.

"I don't know how to tell you this, so I'm just going to tell you," her father blurted suddenly, tearing Julia from her thoughts and memories.

"What?"

"I'm leaving."

She'd known the words were coming, but that didn't stop the wrecking ball from taking a swing at her midsection. She closed her eyes against the pain. "When?"

"I don't know. Soon." He blew out a breath and slicked a hand through his hair. "I'll come back and see you often, I swear I will."

She nodded mutely.

"I tried to keep an honest job here, Julia. I really did. I want to be near you. But I've got this inner call to see the world. It haunts me day and night. Staying here, and working one job, isn't what I was made for.''

Julia knew. It was why her father looked so ragged. The sweet siren of new sights and sounds beckoned. Of course he was going to follow.

''Can I make one request?'' she asked softly.

''Shoot.''

''Bang.''

Her father looked startled for a moment, then laughed.

''Stay for my wedding?''

His eyes grew wide. ''Come again?''

''Well, I'm not positive I can still convince the big lug that just left that I'm marriage material, but he seems to have taken a liking to me. I can't seem to live without him.''

''I'll be there,'' Greg promised.

''Oh, and there's one other thing.''

''Name it.''

''Could you help me move from this awful, lumpy couch to the armchair? I don't have my crutches handy, and my back is killing me.''

She'd only meant for him to give her a hand, but with a wide, endearing smile, her father scooped her into his arms, proving himself in as good a shape as a younger man.

As he gently seated her on the armchair, he paused. ''Can I get you anything before I leave?''

"No," Julia mumbled, feeling suddenly exhausted. Her father's beaming smile was genuine. He really cared for her.

Perhaps it was time to bridge the chasm she'd formed between them and voice what she only now discovered she felt.

"Daddy?" she said as he turned to leave.

"Hmm?" he asked, looking back from his path to the door.

"I love you."

His lips quivered for a moment as he fought for control. Then a lone tear escaped from the corner of his eye and meandered down the lines of his cheek to bank off the crease of his jaw. His cloudy blue eyes cleared, gleaming in a way that made him look years younger than he was.

"I love you, too," her father croaked before dropping to his knees by her side and crushing her in his strong embrace. "Oh, baby, I love you, too."

Chapter Nineteen

Julia had spent the dark hours picturing how Zeke would grin when she told him she loved him, a thought that had sent shivers down her spine, though she'd been toasty warm under her electric blanket.

Like the strong and compassionate man he was, Zeke had willingly stepped out of the way in order for her to pursue what he must have believed in his heart would make her happy.

But now she was going to rectify that error.

"Please help me find Zeke," Julia implored Lakeisha, grabbing her roommate by both hands as she passed the lumpy couch where she was once again ensconced. "I've got to talk to him right away."

"Don't you think you've put him through enough, girl?" Lakeisha asked blatantly. "You know he's in love with you, don't you? Don't hurt him more by chasing after him when you don't mean it."

"Hurt him?" Julia exclaimed. "Hurt him? I want to *marry* the man, not hurt him."

At Lakeisha's astonished look, she nodded. "You're right. I've been an idiot. I've been in love with Zeke for a long time. I was just too foolish to realize it." Her eyes penetrated into Lakeisha's, imploring her to read the honest intensity of her heart.

Her roommate's gaze narrowed, and then she nodded. "Do you know where to find him?"

Julia shook her head. "He could be anywhere."

Where would Zeke go? Her mind blanked. She'd called him, but he was either not home or not answering the phone. The last time she'd tried, the number had come up as disconnected, which is what put her in such a panic now.

She was about to throw her hands up in despair when it suddenly hit her. "The pond behind the church."

"The *pond?*" Lakeisha questioned, sounding as if she believed she hadn't heard Julia correctly. Then, with a dramatic sigh, she shrugged. "Okay, girl. What I won't do for the cause of true love."

It took fifteen minutes for the two women to get Julia down the stairs, into the car, and to make the short drive to the church. Getting to the grove of trees behind the church was another matter. They were hampered at every step by Julia's amateur use of her crutches, particularly when they began moving across the loose-packed snow.

Julia's heart fell as she neared the pond. It was too quiet. Zeke must have gone somewhere else. Her intuition had been wrong.

At this rate she'd never have the opportunity to explain. Her mind explored all of the horrible possibilities. What if he left town before she had a chance to speak to him?

Forget speaking to him. She wanted to plant a kiss on him he'd never forget. One that would leave him wanting more for the rest of his life.

When Lakeisha suggested they return to the car, Julia begged for a few minutes alone.

"You're sure you can make it out here? It's pretty slick."

"I'll be fine. I just need a few minutes alone." To let her heart break in solitude.

"Okay. I'll be waiting for you in the car."

Lakeisha moved off, leaving Julia alone with her thoughts and her crutches.

She sucked in a big gust of crisp, clean air, another by-product of the recent snow. Denver, like most large cities, had a brown cloud of pollution that choked the oxygen out of the air. But with the snow came relief, and for the moment, Julia gloried in the very act of breathing, letting the cool air brush the cobwebs from her head and the hot sting of her heart.

Working her way carefully to a spot near the water's edge, she leaned her head back against the tree, welcoming the feel of the scratchy bark against her scalp.

Her heart turned to God, and she willed herself to pray, to offer her burdens and her shattered heart up to God. Out here, God seemed so much closer, more approachable. She observed His handiwork all around her, from the scratchy pine at her back to the bristling of a chipmunk who had inadvertently run across her path.

When she opened her eyes again, she was amazed to see the outline of Zeke's sturdy frame. She rubbed her eyes to be sure he wasn't a mirage formed from a desperate heart.

He stood at the edge of the pond with his back toward her, his hands thrust into the front pockets of his blue jeans. He didn't have a coat, but seemed oblivious to the frigid winter air.

She slowly became aware that she was trespassing on something infinitely private, and felt her cheeks warm in spite of the fact that her intrusion was unintentional and as yet unnoticed.

She thought he might be praying. Part of her wanted to leave, but something greater compelled her to stay. She sat quietly at the base of the tree and watched him for a moment.

His Rockies cap was pulled low over his brow, complimenting his sharp, bearded profile. He was gazing over the lake, his breath coming in short puffs of white.

He looked so strong and handsome with the winter sunlight forming a background to his fine physique. Her heart swelled with tenderness as she considered what he must be suffering unnecessarily.

He looked so unhappy.

"Zeke," she called quietly, almost afraid to break the silence.

He turned slowly, his big blue eyes widening. "Julia," he gulped. "What are you doing here?

Zeke's heart, already pounding loudly from the exertion of the hike he'd just made, doubled its rate. He smiled grimly and walked to where Julia sat. The skin on his face stung with the flush of effort. The crisp air caused his breath to come out in heavy puffs spewing from his laboring lungs.

It stung, and he was glad.

"Julia," he said in greeting. "I didn't see you."

Though he was flustered by her presence, he struggled not to show it. She was a welcome friend, not an intruder.

She patted the ground next to her. "Have a seat. I'd offer coffee, but I didn't think to bring any."

"Don't mind if I do," he said, flopping down on the snow across from her. He stretched out onto his side and leaned onto his elbow. After a moment, he broke the silence. "What are you up to?"

"I came here looking for you. But when I didn't

see your truck in the lot, I decided I needed a few minutes alone to think,'' she said, her voice earnest.

''I came here to think, as well,'' he admitted gravely. ''Nothing like fresh air to put things in perspective.''

''Me and my pathetic problems,'' Julia lamented.

He reached out and tucked a lock of her hair behind her ear, brushing the soft sweetness of her cheek with his fingers as he did so.

''What's troubling you?'' he asked, his voice unusually low.

''My father, partially,'' she answered, but Zeke didn't think she was telling the whole truth. Her expression was shaded.

''He's a good man,'' Zeke said quietly.

She nodded slowly. ''Yes. I guess I'm beginning to realize that.''

''I've spoken with him several times at HeartBeat.''

''He'll be leaving soon,'' Julia said in a monotone.

Zeke cleared his throat. ''I'm sorry to hear that. Have you worked things out with him?''

''Yes, in a way. I think I'm beginning to understand my father. I don't agree with his methods, but I think I can finally accept him for who and what he is.''

''I'm glad.'' Zeke stroked her arm, offering reassurance. ''I like to see you happy. This thing with your father has taken more out of you than I think you realize.''

''How so?''

''Sometimes the problems we have here on earth affect our relationship with God.''

''That hasn't happened with me,'' Julia immediately protested, and then quickly clamped her mouth closed.

Hadn't she been having problems praying lately? And her priorities were all confused, of that much she was certain, and she hadn't the faintest idea how to fix the problem. And all along, Zeke had known.

She looked across at Zeke, focusing instead on his handsome face. He looked worn, his blue eyes troubled.

''I was thinking about you,'' he said as if in answer to her unspoken question.

Julia's gaze shot to Zeke's face. He had risen to a sitting position, his arms clasped around his knees, and was staring back at her, his features even.

''About me?'' she echoed weakly.

''I just want you to forget all about what I said on Christmas morning, okay?''

''What? Why?''

''It doesn't matter.''

''What do you mean it doesn't matter? Is that why you've had your phone turned off? Because you don't love me anymore?''

He gave her an odd look. ''I didn't have my

phone turned off. You must have called a wrong number.''

Julia looked away as her face flamed. But she couldn't help the words that tumbled from her lips ''I love you, Zeke.''

He stood abruptly, his hands clenched into fists at his side. ''Julia, don't,'' he pleaded, his voice cracking with emotion.

Her words thrown back at her, however unintentionally. She cringed as she fumbled with her crutches in an effort to stand. ''Listen to me,'' she implored, reaching her arms to him. ''It's always been you. I was just too blind to realize it.''

He brushed her hands aside as he walked past her, back up the hill.

''Zeke, please.'' She'd beg if she had to. He'd been through enough pain on her account—it was no wonder he mistrusted her now. But she couldn't very well chase after him, so she had to make do with her words. ''Just hear me out.''

When he froze midstride, she took that as a good sign, and plunged in with the truth. ''I love you. I have for a long time. I had all these foolish plans, and I was all mixed up.''

She ground to a halt.

When he turned, his expression was laced with pain, but Julia could see the hope shining from his clear blue eyes. She allowed all the intensity of her love to flow from her heart and through their locked gazes. Surely he could feel the sincerity of her love.

He smiled in that crooked way he had, and her heart turned over.

"I love you, too," he said, his voice low and raspy.

With a growl of happiness, he pulled her into his warm embrace and kissed her. He marveled at the way his arms fit so perfectly around her, as if they'd been made for each other. But then again, he mused in amazement, they *had* been made for each other.

And if he had his way, she wouldn't spend a day out of his arms, not for the rest of her life.

After a few minutes, Zeke broke the embrace. "We've forgotten something important, sweetheart."

"What?" Julia asked, looking dizzy and rumpled and thoroughly kissed.

Zeke dropped to one knee in the snow, and she clutched her hand to her heart.

"Julia Marie Evans, will you marry me, funny name and all?"

Julia composed her features into an expression of serious contemplation. "Ezekiel Habakkuk Malachi Taylor," she said, a small chuckle escaping her at the mention of his middle names, "I would be honored to become your wife."

He stood and whooped with joy, throwing his Rockies cap into the air, and hardly noticing when it caught up on a high branch, sending a shower of snow to baptize them like rice at a wedding reception. ‘‘Now don’t you go repeating that name in public,’’ he warned.

Julia wiggled back into the comfort of his arms. ‘‘Well, there is one way you could keep me from talking,’’ she suggested coyly.

He laughed and obliged her upturned lips.

They stood silently for a minute, enjoying the quiet perfection of the moment. ‘‘Julia, sweetheart?’’ Zeke whispered into the freshness her hair.

‘‘Hmm?’’

‘‘Is there anyone you’d like me to…you know, ask…I mean, for a blessing on our marriage?’’

Julia leaned back and smiled full into Zeke’s face. ‘‘This won’t come as a surprise, I don’t think, but it would be nice to ask…my father.’’

Epilogue

"Julia, girl, you outdid yourself," Lakeisha said with a happy chuckle.

"I'll say," agreed Greg Evans, who was seated in a wicker rocking chair, contentedly rocking a newborn baby in the corner of the room. After two years, Julia wasn't sure she'd still be in contact with her father, and yet here he was, sharing her joy. *Their joy.*

"Where did you get her name, anyway?" Lakeisha asked, breaking into Julia's thoughts. "Esther Naomi Ruth. It's beautiful. Long, but beautiful."

Julia's heart welled at the thought of her newborn, and the man who was now the proud father. She shared a knowing smile with Zeke.

Zeke's arms were also laden with a newborn baby.

"Or *his* name, either," Lakeisha continued, reaching out to jiggle the baby boy's hand. He gurgled, and Lakeisha chuckled.

"Matthew Luke," Zeke pronounced heartily.

Julia rejoiced that her dear friend—and her father—shared this special day with her and her beaming husband. The secret of the names, they'd keep between the two of them.

Lakeisha kissed the boy's forehead, then turned and kissed little Esther's fair cheek.

"Esther Ruth Naomi and Matthew Luke," Julia pronounced with a mother's smile. "Twin blessings. And that's the gospel truth."

* * * * *

Dear Reader,

Have you ever done the right thing for the wrong reason?

Julia Evans wanted to serve God with her whole heart, but in her zeal, in her reliance on her own abilities and resources, she was tempted to do God's work on her own. In the process, she almost missed God's best for her!

I don't know about you, but I often get so busy that I don't wait on the Lord. I jump from project to project like a wild kangaroo, and never take the time to rest and seek God's best for my life. Yet it is when Christ works through my weaknesses that I am truly strong.

I hope you'll take a moment now to stop and wait upon the Lord. Depend upon God, dear reader. Only through His power can we be effective for Him.

I pray God's best for you, today and always.

I love to hear from my readers. Let me know what you thought about Zeke and Julia's story, and how you've sought God's best in your life. My address is P.O. Box 28140 #16, Lakewood, CO 80228-3108.

God's Best,

Deb Kastner

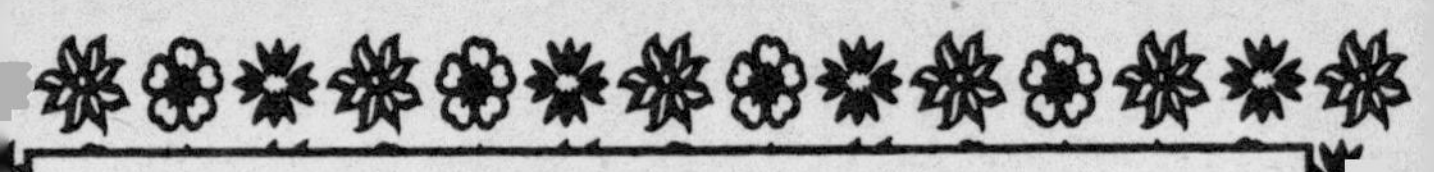